HAND IN HAND

Edited by Twyla Beth Lambert

Cover Art by Ashley Aarons/AmaArt Studios

Cover Design by Fresh Design

Print ISBN 978-1-945419-54-6

Ebook ISBN 978-1-945419-55-3

Library of Congress Control Number 2020930171

HAND IN HAND

KATIE PROCTOR

FAWKES PRESS

For Grandma Norma, who tells her stories so well they become part of us

NOVEMBER 1940

Seven-year-old Hazel Jackson clutched Papa's hand and held a scarf up to her face to protect her cheeks from the biting wind. He was walking fast, with purpose, though she wasn't quite sure where they were going. What she did know was that they were on their way for Papa to vote.

Hazel shivered, remembering Ma Maybelle's warning at the breakfast table just that morning. "Be careful Willie, son. You know them white folk get all jittery on voting day."

"Aw, Ma, don't get me down, now. Voting's somethin' I gotta do. Can't help make no changes, can't make life better for us if we don't vote."

To that, she'd said, "I know it, Willie. Just... be careful's all."

Now, almost yelling to be heard above the cry of the wind, Hazel said, "Why do white folk get all jittery, Papa?"

"Hazel, my girl, some of them white folk don't want us colored folk to vote. They're scared they gonna lose their power. But how can they, when all them politicians're white? Still, a man's gotta vote. And that's what I'm gonna do."

Mama had put up a big fight when Papa said he was taking

Hazel with him—not being safe and all, not knowing what the white folk would do when he tried to cast his ballot. But in the end, he'd won out—saying she needed to see democracy in action, that his own children would grow up to exercise their rights—and Hazel had followed Papa out, proud to be holding his strong hand.

Papa wore his best suit, freshly cleaned and ironed. He shaved his face, too, and wore a tidy cap over his head full of tight curls. Hazel never remembered her Papa getting so dressed up for a walk to downtown. He looked like he did on Sundays for church.

When City Hall came into view, Hazel's chest felt like someone had reached in and was squeezing it tight. There was a line: white men and a few white women, all of them bundled in long coats. The cold front had come unexpectedly, and on voting day, no less. There was not one other person with dark skin like Hazel's or Papa's in sight.

"You sure about this, Papa?" Hazel asked, her eyes wide.

"Yes, Hazel. I am here to vote, and I intend to do just that. Now, if things get ugly, you run, okay? Fast as you can, right back home. You hear?"

"Yes, Papa." His words forced her to suck in a breath of cold air, and a shiver crawled up her spine before she let it out.

As they walked closer to the line, Hazel could feel the white folks' stares as they bore into her. She could hear whispers and coughs as they took their place at the end. The man right in front of Hazel looked hard at them and then took a large, exaggerated step forward to put some distance between them. Papa looked straight ahead, resolute.

The line inched forward, quicker than Hazel would've guessed, but it was cold and she supposed folks wanted to get on home. No one said a word to Papa until they had reached the steps and a red-faced man walked right up to them. Hazel squeezed Papa's hand harder.

"Go find your own place to vote. No Negroes allowed here, boy!"

Papa smiled tightly down at Hazel to assure her everything was fine and then looked the man right in the face as he spoke, "Sir, I got a Constitutional right to vote, and I aim to do it. Ain't no other place in town to vote and you know it."

A different man stepped closer to Papa and spat in his face. "Then I guess you ain't voting today. Now get." Another man nearby growled, "You people shouldn't even have the vote." Others in line agreed with loud calls of "Yessir!" and "Here, here!"

Papa, letting go of Hazel's hand, wiped his face calmly with a handkerchief—for even in the cold, beads of sweat had formed on his face—and stood his ground. Nobody spoke until two more important-looking men in suits came out to investigate.

One of them walked up to Papa, looking him up and down with a devilish grin spread across his face. "Okay, darkie. You got poll tax money?"

"Yes, sir," Papa said and held out an envelope, full of two week's worth of wages. There had also been an argument at home about this. Two week's worth of wages could buy a lot for their family. But Papa had saved it, over months, for just this day. Hazel hadn't seen anyone else pay any money to vote.

The man took it, counted every single bill slowly and deliberately, then counted again. "Okay, boy, now all's you have to do is pass this here literacy test"—he waved a paper covered with very small print in Papa's face—"and *then* we'll see about you voting."

Papa stiffened, but looked down at Hazel. "S'okay, go on home, like we talked. This may take a while, Hazel-girl." Hazel shook her head, there was no way she was leaving Papa there. She was starting to think the only reason they hadn't done worse to him was because she was there.

"No, Papa, I don't mind waiting. I'll stay."

She heard a woman behind her cough and say, not-so-quietly to her friend, "Can't even control his insolent child." The words burned into Hazel's very soul, she was never disrespectful—that was her brother Willie Jr.'s job.

"Well—you coming or not, boy?" the man asked. "Or are you too stupid? What's the matter? Can't read?"

Papa bit his lip, hesitating a bit too long, because at that moment, the man shoved Papa and he fell down the steps backward. Folks nearby moved out of his way but made no move to help him up. Hazel cried out and ran to his side, freezing when she saw the man pull out a shiny, silver, sharp-looking knife. Papa looked at her with a panic in his eye and said firmly but quietly, "Hazel. Go on home." Then his panic subsided and with more determination than she'd ever seen, he finished, "I'll see you when I come home. I love you."

She didn't want to leave him, but she knew Papa was real serious. She waited until he stood, hugged his leg, whispered, "I love you, too, Papa," and then turned toward home. The last thing she heard was Papa clear his throat and say, "Okay, sir, I'm ready for that there test."

As she passed the folks in line, though, Hazel spied a little girl about her age with wild red hair and a face full of freckles, watching Hazel with wide eyes and a hand over her mouth. Hazel didn't have time to give her another thought as she ran, but those bright red curls were burned into her memory for years to come.

1

LILLIAN JOSEPHINE WAGNER

JUNE 1945

Lily never saw her daddy cry until the day a dirty red brick shattered the front window of the store. She didn't even know it had happened until she got home from school, the last day before summer vacation, but that day marked the start of the most memorable summer of Lily's life.

The day began like any regular school day, with Lily trying to wake Marianne and having no luck.

"Go away," her sister grumbled and rolled over to face the wall. Marianne's long blonde hair flowed with a perfect wave, even when she slept. This made her look almost angelic, a thought that made Lily chuckle. Her sister was anything but angelic. She was fifteen and didn't care much for school. Or for Lily, for that matter.

Unlike Marianne, Lily couldn't wait to gobble her breakfast and get to school. She'd been through lots of last days before, but the significance of this particular last day was not lost on her. It was her last day of elementary school; she'd officially be a seventh grader by the afternoon.

Leaving her sister to sleep, Lily bounded down the stairs

and found Maybelle in the kitchen, a whirl of activity. Maybelle wore a white apron over a smooth blue dress that hugged her slim waist. Her dark brown hair was tied up in a tight bun and wrapped in a purple scarf, but not so much that Lily couldn't spy the strands of white that peeked out. Maybelle's sturdy, ebony-colored hands were in constant motion. Lily took a deep breath, overwhelmed by some of her favorite smells: buttery biscuits in the oven, Mother's coffee brewing, sausage crackling in the cast iron skillet.

"Mornin', Miss Lily," Maybelle said. "Your hair's a right mess, girl." She patted Lily on the head, smoothing down some of the bright red frizz, and gave Lily a glass of fresh-squeezed orange juice.

"Aw, Maybelle. I was sweatin' up there! It's gonna be a hot one!" Lily boosted herself up onto the green formica countertop and started helping Maybelle pack lunches for school. "Hey, Miss Lily, I ever tell you 'bout Martha?"

"No, I don't think so. Who's Martha?"

"Only the best cook in the entire state of South Carolina. Martha worked in the Big House at the plantation and taught me everything I know. You know them mashed potatoes you love? The ones smooth as butter but a little chunky in just the right way? Martha's who taught me that. Those collards, too. I wouldn't touch a collard green 'less Martha made it, that's the truth!" Maybelle's hands seemed to move as fast as her mouth, whisking the flour into the sausage drippings and taking the biscuits out of the oven.

Lily smiled, spreading mayonnaise on Maybelle's home-made bread before adding thick slices of honey ham. "What made 'em so good?"

"Oh, child. You know the secret ingredient. S'always bacon!" The joy coming from Maybelle's laugh filled up the whole kitchen. It was one of Lily's favorite sounds in the whole world.

"Of course, how could I forget?"

"And did I ever tell you 'bout the time I found the rat in the flour sack?" Maybelle's voice rang out.

"Nope!" Lily said. Of course, she'd heard the story loads of times, but she so loved to hear Maybelle tell it.

"... I never saw a white lady so scared in my life!" Maybelle finished just as Marianne and June, the eldest Wagner sister, finally stumbled into the kitchen. Marianne raised an eyebrow in Maybelle's direction, and the slightest hint of a smile played on June's lips but was gone in an instant. Lily couldn't help but notice then that Maybelle's whole demeanor changed, the silliness of her story gone. Mother swept in next, a modest pink cotton house dress swishing around her ankles. Lily slid down from the countertop and smoothed her nightgown.

"Mornin', Missus Wagner," Maybelle said.

"Good morning, Maybelle." Mother picked up her steaming cup of coffee and wrapped her hands around it as if the dark liquid inside was some kind of magic elixir. Lily had no earthly idea how Mother could sip such a hot drink on a day this muggy.

"Did Clarke leave for the store yet?" Mother asked Maybelle as they all settled into the dining room.

"Yes'm, he did. 'Bout ten minutes ago." Maybelle set a plate of hot biscuits and creamy sausage gravy in front of each girl.

Mother nodded and continued to sip her coffee while the girls ate in silence.

"Okay, girls. Time to get ready. Now don't forget to look your best. We can't have the boys forgetting the Wagner girls this summer!" Mother said with a teasing smile after their plates had been all but licked clean.

Lily couldn't help stealing a glance at June, who joined her in rolling their eyes. As if the boys paid any attention to Lily beyond her hot pitching arm and her uncanny ability to catch the biggest fish in the creek or to June beyond needing help with homework. Everyone knew Marianne was the only Wagner sister turning the heads of the Mayfield boys, a fact both Lily and June had agreed they didn't care a lick about.

The unfortunate odor of bodies affected by the already-stifling heat reminded Lily of dirty gym socks and stung her eyes as she and her classmates piled into the gym for the end-of-year assembly. She had heard there would be a visit from the superintendent and wondered absently what he would say. Elsie and Francis were already sitting on the bleachers, their foreheads almost touching as they whispered and giggled. Lily sat down next to them, looking around for Beau.

That boy, always late, Lily thought, shaking her head, as she glanced at the clock. Just seconds before the heavy gym doors slammed shut, Beau slid into the seat next to Lily, his face dirty and brown hair tousled. While this might have alarmed someone else, Lily smiled at the predictability of her friend; this was how he always looked, only clean on Sundays.

"Hey," Beau whispered, his voice urgent. "What happened at the store?"

Lily turned to look at him. "Whaddya mean?"

He shrugged. "I just saw lotsa people crowded around this morning, on my way back from digging for worms at the creek. But I was late, couldn't stop."

As the superintendent made his way to the basketball court below, a restless silence fell over the gym.

"I'm sure it's nothing," Lily waved him off, annoyed that

he'd gone to the creek without her. "Now hush, I wanna hear this."

Beau shrugged and turned his attention to the jolly, silver-haired man with rosy cheeks who reminded Lily of Santa Claus. Sweat stained the underarms and collar of his seersucker suit. He grinned as he stepped up to the rickety podium, steadied himself, and dabbed at his forehead with a handkerchief.

"Well, well, well. You've made it to the end of another successful school year. Your teachers have told me how hard you worked and how much you learned. And summer is such a fine time, especially for those of you moving on to junior high next year. Your time here is done, and I know it might be a little frightening to think of what lies ahead."

Excited whispers floated around the gym, and Lily could almost taste the energy in the room, it was so alive. No one could wait for this day to end and their summer to begin.

"But I believe the most important thing is your education. And sometimes, I know, we can all get a bit lazy during the summer. So, I'm here to kick off the annual summer reading contest."

A few people said, "Yes!" or "Oh yeah!" But Lily sighed, feeling silly for getting excited for an announcement she should've known was coming. It was just the summer reading contest. *Bo-ring.* June had won it the summer before she went to seventh grade, but Lily had never paid it much attention. She read well enough in school when she had to, but summer was for all kinds of other things.

"The winner will receive a prize, and we will also have prizes for the second and third place readers."

Beulah May Porter's hand shot into the air. An audible groan rippled through the crowd, prompting a frown from Mr.

Edwards. Beulah May was the smartest girl in school, and she never let anyone forget it.

"Excuse me, sir, but how long do the books have to be? And how do we make sure that people," she paused to look condescendingly at her classmates, "actually read them?"

"All good questions, young lady, I was just getting there."

Beulah May put her nose in the air, clearly pleased with herself, sat up straight, and leaned forward to listen to the answers. Lily suspected that everyone, including Beulah May herself, knew she would win the contest. Even now, she cradled a book like a precious baby and a tall stack sat in a pile at her feet. *Who brings a stack of books to the last day of school?* Lily thought. *Someone else needs to win that contest.* It briefly occurred to her that maybe she could be the one to do it, but only for a second, before thoughts of ball games and fishing once again occupied her mind.

Mr. Edwards said something about Miss Nora, the town librarian, keeping count and the annual end-of-summer picnic and then strode off the stage with a flicker of a wave and a grin. Lily elbowed Beau and they both glanced at Beulah May, who began loudly flipping the pages of one of her books as if she wanted everyone to notice she was starting right away. Beau rolled his eyes at Lily and they both laughed.

LILY AND BEAU walked home side by side, her lunch pail swinging, occasionally hitting him in the leg. Neither of them realized that the sun had stopped beating down relentlessly, that the wind had shifted, that the clouds were dark, creating a gloom that was rare for June.

"Whaddya think about ol' Beulah May?" Beau asked.

"What about her?"

"She's so certain she's gonna win that contest. But I wish she wouldn't. She could stand to lose something now and again."

"She sure could. All that huffing today made my blood boil. Still, she'll probably win anyhow."

"Hey, Lil? Let's do it. The contest, I mean. You and me. Let's beat her."

Lily's jaw dropped. "Seriously, Beau? But... fishin' and kick the can and baseball... I'd rather do all that."

"C'mon Lily," he begged. "We can still do all that, just throw in some reading!"

She knew Beau liked to read, especially *The Hardy Boys* books, but also that he liked to keep that particular detail to himself. This sudden competitive spark threw Lily for a loop.

"Please?" Beau nudged her gently, but she had been mid-stride and nearly stumbled into the blooming crepe myrtle that signaled they were almost home.

Straightening up, she said, "Okay fine. Let's go to the library in the mor—"

Her words were cut off when Beau stopped abruptly in front of his house and threw out an arm to stop Lily as well.

A tall holly bush blocked their view, but Lily could hear three or four men shouting on the porch. Beau put a finger to his lips and they stood still, listening. Mr. Adams's voice was the loudest, but the other men sounded just as angry. Lily wondered what they had to be so irate about. The war seemed to be coming to an end; Germany had just surrendered and it looked like Japan would be close behind them. What else in sleepy little Mayfield could get them so worked up?

Lily couldn't make out exact words, but she heard things like "Negro" and "Jim Crow" and "now they're all gonna do it."

Beau stiffened and looked at Lily, his eyes wide. Even though he was Beau's pa, Lily was frightened of Mr. Adams.

He appeared to be a quiet family man, his suits always clean and pressed and his hair always slicked back, but she got a weird feeling in her stomach every time he was around.

"Who's Jim Crow?" Lily whispered to Beau, who shrugged but put a finger to his lips to shush her. It was too late, though.

The voices quieted, as if someone had ordered them to hush. Heavy footsteps stomped down the porch steps. Lily froze. There was nowhere to hide and neither one could have run at that moment. A pair of pale hands pushed back a section of the hedge and Mr. Adams appeared. Lily grabbed Beau's hand, and he didn't even try to wriggle out of it like usual.

"Git on outta here, girl. Don't you know better than to eavesdrop on grown folk? And you, boy," he growled, turning on Beau, "git in the house." He barely hid the disgust he surely felt at being overheard.

Lily couldn't get away from him fast enough; she ran into her own yard and up the steps, with only one glance at Beau, who hung his head as he followed his father.

Once inside the house, Lily was surprised to see Mother and Daddy both home; it was still early in the day. She couldn't wait to tell Daddy what she'd just overheard and ask him about this Jim Crow person; Daddy knew everything. But when Lily peered into the kitchen, she saw June and Marianne there, too.

"Lily Jo, darlin', come sit down." Her father's tone was light but serious in a way that told her she should do as he said. The incident with Mr. Adams left her mind, and her questions died in her throat.

"The store was vandalized today, Lily Jo."

"Wh... what do you mean?" she stammered. It was then that she took a good look at Daddy. His eyes were red. They looked tired. He looked older.

"A brick was thrown through the front window, there's

glass everywhere. And someone painted a rather unkind message on the door."

Lily looked at her sisters; they had obviously heard all of this already. June looked down at the table, and Marianne's face was red—her mouth twisted in a strange sort of frown, but they both remained quiet.

"No one was hurt, thankfully, as it was done in the night. But it was still quite the shock," he said softly as a lone tear rolled down his cheek. He brushed it away quickly.

"But..." she couldn't help herself, "Why, Daddy? Why'd someone do that?"

He looked down at his hands. "Because, yesterday I took the Whites Only sign off the front door. That's why."

2

HAZEL CLEMENTINE JACKSON

Hazel awoke in the stifling heat next to her sisters who were snoring lightly. Their blanket had been thrown aside and the straw mattress was soaked in sweat. Even so, she must have slept hard because she hadn't heard her grandmother, Ma Maybelle, get up and leave for town where she worked for that white family.

Hazel woke Glory first then the others and tiptoed into the stuffy kitchen where she heated a single pork chop and some leftover grits for breakfast. Mornings were her favorite. She loved being in the quiet kitchen alone, preparing breakfast and packing lunches, before all the chaos erupted and her siblings started shouting and demanding things. Just as she was thinking this, Willie Jr. and Tremaine burst into the kitchen and practically plowed into the girls as they raced to the table.

"Aw, grits again, Hazel? Really?" Willie Jr. whined.

"Hush up and eat," Hazel replied matter-of-factly, ignoring his complaint.

Willie Jr. grumbled, "Yes, Mama," and Hazel shot him a look. It wasn't like she wanted to take care of him all the time.

But their mama left before the sun came up to get to the hotel on time.

Hallie came in a second later. She dragged baby Nell behind her, both rubbing the sleep out of their eyes. Nell squealed for Hazel to pick her up, so she finished making lunches with Nell on her hip. Hallie sidled up next to Glory and ate her breakfast in silence.

Glory was only a year younger than Hazel, and of all the Jackson siblings, Hazel felt closest to her. It often fell on both of them to care for the younger ones, and the two had perfected their morning duties so that everything worked like a well-oiled machine. Glory woke Nell and Tremaine and helped them dress while Hazel handled the meals.

Hazel wondered if sweet Hallie knew that both of the older girls would need to work this summer. She decided not to tell her just yet. One look at Glory told Hazel she was thinking the same thing.

"When does Papa get home?" Hallie asked.

"He's coming for a couple days this weekend," was Hazel's reply. "Mama'll be happy."

"Me, too," Hallie said quietly.

"Papa gonna take me and Willie fishin'!" Tremaine piped in. Hazel said a silent prayer that Papa would be able to keep the promise. Lately, when he came home on weekends, he was so tired. The effort he had to put forth working the fields with only one good arm exhausted him. He'd lost so much in the war —an arm, yes, but also his bright smile, his boisterous laughter, his flirtatious grins for Mama. They'd all been so relieved the day he walked back in the house that Hazel wondered if she was the only one who noticed the change in him. She still managed to get a smile out of him now and again, but it was rare, and it seemed to shine a little less than before.

"Maybe he'll bring us a chocolate bar!"

"Don't get your hopes up, Hallie-girl. Though it'd be nice," Glory said.

"And Ma Maybelle'd love him forever," Tremaine added, making them all laugh.

Hazel liked when Papa was home. He seemed to fill up the house like it had been completely empty before, and even the walls seemed to breathe a little easier. Mama was happier when he was there, too, so Hazel knew they'd be celebrating this weekend.

After the little ones were taken care of, Hazel got ready to leave for school, slipping into a freshly ironed gray dress, soft and faded but clean. A quick glance in the mirror showed a girl with striking golden eyes and a smooth complexion, a girl not quite ready to grow all the way up yet. She couldn't tell if she was pretty, or even if she cared. But she loved school more than anything, so she flashed herself a dimpled smile and tied a red plaid scarf around her thick braids.

The screen door creaked open and Miss Essie came inside just as Hazel stepped out of the bathroom. Miss Essie wore a long, sleeveless house dress and her graying hair was tied up in a colorful scarf. She fanned her face with an old church pamphlet and sat down in the only chair in the front room.

"Lunch is in the kitchen, Miss Essie," Hazel told her. "And Nell's all cleaned up."

"Thank you, child." Miss Essie smiled the kind of smile that showed all the lines around her eyes. Hazel knew she was lucky that Miss Essie had agreed to watch the younger ones. If it weren't for her, Hazel probably would've had to quit school to help with them, like a couple of her classmates had done already.

Hazel picked up her lunch and made sure to grab the book Miss Grace had lent her. She needed to give it back today. Hazel took a minute to look at it; yellowed pages, brown leather cover, well-worn because it had been well-loved. And there was something satisfying about feeling the weight of it in her hands. Reading was the way Hazel could move beyond the four walls of her home. She could travel, solve mysteries, be part of big adventures in faraway places. Books helped her imagine worlds that could be, things she could go on to do, people she'd never have the chance to meet otherwise. She was so glad Miss Grace felt the same way. Their shared loved of books felt like a safe, secret place Hazel always knew she belonged.

With a sigh, she tucked the book into her bag and followed the others out the door.

When they reached the run-down school building, Hazel left her siblings and skipped to her classroom. As usual, she got there before the other students who milled around the yard, delaying the start of the day as long as they could. When Hazel reached the closed door of Miss Grace's classroom, she skidded to a halt, smoothed down her dress, and took a deep breath before she walked in.

"I'm glad you came a little early today, Hazel!" Miss Grace beamed. "I have something special for you, for our last day."

As Hazel approached Miss Grace, she made sure to take in the classroom, probably for the last time. The windows were old and dingy, the desks wobbly and mismatched. The metal chairs made an awful creaking sound. None of them had legs of even length, so they rocked from side to side. During the last nine months, Hazel had spent the majority of her waking moments in this room, and now she thought how strange it was to know a place so intimately for so long, and then one day to never exist in it again. She might see it another time, but she knew it would never feel the same as it did right this minute.

Hazel handed Miss Grace the book she needed to return, and Miss Grace set it on her desk. She reached into her bag and pulled out a small package, wrapped in the front page of the *Mayfield Gazette*. Hazel's eyes lit up; she loved presents. Carefully taking it in her hands, she looked up at Miss Grace's twinkling smile. Hazel pulled at the newspaper to unwrap the gift, and her eyes filled with tears when she spotted the corner of a book.

A real, live book.

All hers.

"I was in Pearl's last week and saw this book. I just knew you had to have it. I want you to read it this summer and come back and visit sometime to tell me what you think, you hear?"

Hazel nodded and closed her eyes, trying to keep tears from rolling down her face.

"Oh, Miss Grace, I can't take this. It musta cost a fortune."

"Don't you think on it, Hazel. Besides, Miss Pearl doesn't even put prices on some of her books. She takes what you have to give."

"Really?" Hazel asked.

"Lord knows how that woman stays in business, but I guess even in the worst of times, folks still need good stories to lift their spirits. And it helps she's the only bookseller for miles."

Now the tears fell, and Hazel let them. Miss Grace smiled and reached out to gently pat her hand.

Hazel looked down to examine the book. It had a beautiful hardback cover, full of color and promise. And, most exciting of all, on the cover was a shiny silver sticker, letting the world know it had won a Newbery Honor. Hazel had heard of these books before but had never read one, and never had one to call her own. Now, in her very hands, was *The Hundred Dresses* by Eleanor Estes. Hazel didn't know how she'd make it to the end of the day without sneaking a peek.

"It's not about a colored girl, now," Miss Grace said. "But I think you'll still find you have a lot in common with the main character, with Wanda. She's a special girl with a special strength, just like you. Wanda is a quiet kind of hero, but a hero nonetheless. You'll see."

Hazel furrowed her brow. She'd never thought about heroes being quiet before. In most of the stories she'd read, the heroes were strong or brave or had big voices that people listened to. For this reason, Hazel had kind of figured she'd never be much of a hero. She preferred the quiet, reading and writing about heroes instead.

"I know just what you're thinking," Miss Grace said with a knowing smile. "But trust me on this one, we need all kinds of heroes in this world. And that's why I picked this book especially for you."

Hazel nodded and gently rewrapped the book and slid it into her bag, trembling with excitement and just a smidge of disbelief.

"Thank you, Miss Grace," was all she could manage.

As she watched the other students pour loudly into the classroom, the significance of this place and the lessons Miss Grace had taught her there weighed heavily, made her feet feel firmly planted to their spot, unwilling to move.

In this room, Miss Grace had told them about brave colored folks like Frederick Douglass and read aloud lyrical poetry by Langston Hughes and short stories by Zora Neale Hurston. Hazel remembered the day they cut Mr. Tucker, Hannah's papa, down from that tree, how Miss Grace had said nothing, but just rocked Hannah back and forth while the rest of them watched, frozen. And she'd never forget Miss Grace's tears as she told them about the men in white hoods who had burned a cross in her front yard when she was only twelve, all because her father had smiled at a white woman on the street. When those same men vandalized the African Methodist Episcopal church just this March, Miss Grace had taken the class outside for some fresh air and didn't teach a single thing all day. Instead, they had spread out with their faces towards the sun, eyes closed, and listened to Miss Grace's strong voice read story after story of hope and courage.

Hazel's heart ached to think of how much she'd miss her teacher. She'd never find another one like Miss Grace.

3

LILY

The Wagners sat together at the table for a while in silence, the only sound a ding from the oven, telling them the dinner Maybelle had prepared was done. Mother got up to take it out, then returned.

Lily spoke first. "But Daddy, why'd you do that? Colored folks still come in the store. They just know to use the back door."

Her sisters and Mother looked at him, eager to hear the answer. Lily's question hung in the air while Daddy ran a hand through his salt-and-pepper hair and removed his thick coke-bottle glasses, the ones Lily loved because they'd kept him out of the fighting overseas.

"I know, Lily Jo. I didn't tell you girls this, but there was an incident day before last." He paused, and even Mother looked up, surprised. "An older colored man—I think the fella's name was Clyde—must have gotten confused in the heat of the day because he tried to come through the front door. Well, Butch Gordon saw him and there was a little scuffle. Butch ended up pulling his revolver out of his pocket and pointing it right at Clyde, who by then was on the ground."

Lily gasped. She couldn't believe it. A gun? Just for trying to go in a door? She knew who Butch was; she was sure his voice had been one of the angry men on Beau's porch earlier that afternoon.

"I ran out there just in time to hear Butch threaten Clyde, but after a while was able to get him to calm down. I don't think Butch would've really hurt the man, but you can't be too careful. After he went inside, I helped Clyde up and told him he best head on home. I wish I would've done more, but I'm just so tired of all of it. We're fighting the Germans and we're fighting the Japanese, too. Didn't seem right fighting our own neighbors here." His voice trailed off, deep in thought, and Lily asked, "But... what'll happen now, Daddy?"

"We clean up the mess and keep on going, I guess. There isn't anything else to do, really."

Lily nodded, but said nothing.

Marianne could not hold it in a second longer. "That's a real sad story and all, but Daddy, how could you *do* this to us? Do you *know* what this is going to mean for me? They won't elect a Negro-loving man's daughter to homecoming court! What will the people at the church say? Our friends? What if... oh no. I won't be able to show my face at the pool or the youth gatherings. My summer is *ruined*! Oh, Daddy, how *could* you?"

She was in a full-on tantrum now, face red, hands flailing, completely unaware of the shock on the faces of the rest of her family. June looked horrified at her sister's outburst, but still said nothing, looking to Daddy for a response.

Mother pursed her lips while she dished out the meatloaf and potatoes and peas, and Lily couldn't help but wonder if Mother and Daddy had already had this exact discussion.

Mother was, after all, head of the United Methodist Women and had a certain reputation to uphold.

"And furthermore." Marianne was not finished, apparently. "What about business? How are white folks gonna feel having to walk inside the same door as the coloreds? We can't go through another time like the Depression, we just *can't*, Daddy!"

Marianne stared, refusing to eat, even though everyone else took small, quiet bites, the scraping of silverware on china the only noise in the room. Daddy—refusing to be admonished by his middle child, and the most spoiled one at that—wiped his mouth and then said, in a calm and measured voice, "Sometimes, Marianne, we have to do the right thing for other people, and not just think about ourselves. Colored folks are my customers too, and they have just as much right to feed their families quality food like we sell. We may lose some folks for a bit, but they'll come back when they get tired of driving all the way to Felton for groceries. If not, we'll get a little creative. You have anyone say anything impolite to you, just send 'em on down to the store. We'll get things straightened out." His words sounded light, but his tone was serious.

Lily could tell Marianne did not appreciate his answer, but she seemed to understand that Daddy was unwilling to discuss it further, because she put on her best pout, crossed her arms, and said nothing else.

WHEN THEY HAD FINISHED dinner and were happily eating cold creamy bites of Maybelle's peach custard, Daddy asked, "Well, girls, how was the last day of school?"

Marianne rolled her eyes like she couldn't bother discussing such a boring topic. June opened her mouth, most likely to start her usual tirade on the fact that it didn't make sense for school to take a summer holiday. They weren't exactly farmers, why such a long break? But they'd all heard the rant before and it tended to go on for some time, so Lily spoke up before June could utter a single syllable.

"The superintendent came to see us today," she said quietly, unsure of how excited she should be, given the circumstances. But Daddy nodded, encouraging her to continue. "He kicked off the summer reading contest. And," she added, "Beau wants us to do it. He wants one of us to beat ol' Beulah May Porter. But I don't know about all that. I guess it might feel good to win something."

Beulah May had gotten under her skin. Someone needed to show her she wasn't the very best at everything.

Daddy said, "You'll do great, Lily Jo," at the same time Mother said, "I'm sure there are many strong readers."

Marianne spoke up again, her voice less shrill than before but her whiny tone the same. "Reading? That's what you're excited about? What a silly thing to bother with. I mean, whoever made a friend because of a book? And furthermore, whoever got a *husband* because of one?"

Daddy gave her a stern look. "Marianne, whatever your opinion may be, let's be happy for Lily Jo and encourage her as much as we can. I'm sure Mr. Edwards just wants children reading so they keep learning over the summer. It's so darn hot already, reading makes a perfect pastime. And, it wouldn't hurt you to crack open a book occasionally."

Lily flashed a grateful smile at Daddy as Marianne scowled; he'd always been her biggest champion.

THAT EVENING, Lily picked up one of June's old *Nancy Drew* books, and was reading in her room alone when she heard a sound on her window, almost like a fat raindrop. Not thinking much of it, she turned back to her book. But then there was another *plink* and another, and she swore she heard someone speak her name. She walked over to the window, pulled up the glass, and stuck her head out. Down below, she saw Beau standing in the grassy area that separated their properties holding a handful of small pebbles.

"Lily, wouldja come down here for a minute? I got something I need to tell you."

"But why didn't you just knock on the door like always?"

He looked down at his feet. Lily could tell something wasn't right. "Hang on, I'll be right there."

When she got down to Beau, he still wouldn't look her in the eye. "Pa says I'm not to see you anymore."

The words hit Lily like a ton of bricks.

"Whaddya mean?" she asked, choking on the knot that had formed in her throat in one second flat. She wasn't sure she'd heard him correctly. How could he say such a thing?

"He says your daddy's a... well... he used a not very nice word to say your daddy likes the coloreds too much and he doesn't want me hanging around here anymore."

"But Beau," Lily said, holding back tears, "we've been friends since I can remember."

"I know. Pa's real mad, though."

Lily's heart raced and she felt the blood rise to her cheeks. She thought of her brave father inside, worrying about his store and his customers. "Oh, your pa's just a mean old grouch. Besides, we're kids. What do we have to do with any of it?" she asked, raising her voice.

"Shhh," Beau warned, looking around. "Listen, we can still be friends. Just not here. We'll have to meet at the library or the creek. We can still do the contest together. We just gotta make it look like we ain't friends."

She couldn't help it. It was like someone else took control of her hands. She shoved Beau so hard he fell back. "You just do whatever you need to, Beaumont Lee Adams!" she spat out his full name, like a mother admonishing a naughty child. Then she turned her back on him and marched back to her front yard. Glancing back just once, she saw her friend sink down into the grass, his head in his hands.

———

THAT NIGHT, Lily found she could not sleep—too many thoughts floating around and around in her mind. Daddy had never said much about the Whites Only sign. She supposed he had hung it there because all the other businesses in Mayfield had done the same. Matter of fact, she didn't think she'd ever heard him say anything about colored folk or white folk or get involved in any of the town matters or politics.

No, that's not true, she thought.

In the silence with only Marianne's light snoring as company, Lily's mind flashed to a memory, one she must've worked hard to forget. But it came back to her now as vividly as if it had happened just the day before. She was young—maybe seven?—and remembered being bundled up against a cold wind. Daddy had told her he needed to run a quick errand and he wanted her to go with him. So they headed out, walking. They didn't take the car out of the shed much then; gasoline was too expensive. When they reached the ivy-covered City Hall building, Lily saw that a line had formed on the steps. She read the sign and asked, "It's voting day?"

"Yes, Lily Jo, we are here to vote."

"What are you voting for, Daddy?"

"Well, now... it's my responsibility to elect a president I believe in, someone who will help our country. The man I am voting for today is Mr. Franklin Delano Roosevelt. He's a good man. And you share his birthday! That is something special, Lily Jo."

She grinned at her daddy and held her head high.

A loud commotion caught their attention, a red-faced man yelling angrily. Lily looked toward the end of the line and Daddy put an arm around her shoulder. Men shouted at a colored man, "Go find your own place to vote, no Negroes allowed here, boy!"

When they pushed him, he stumbled down a couple steps and fell into the dirt. Lily turned to put her face into Daddy's body, not wanting to see what happened next, but then she saw a little colored girl kneel down by the man, and she couldn't look away. She had to have been his daughter, come to vote with her own daddy, just like she had.

Lily felt Daddy's arm twitch, like he was about to move forward and help the man, but his feet stayed firmly planted where they were.

The colored man whispered something to his daughter and then stood up, saying something to the men that got drowned out by the wind. Then the little girl squeezed his leg and left him, her eyes faced determinedly away from City Hall. She locked eyes with Lily for just a second before she took off running.

But the colored man stood his ground, and soon, he entered the building. "Stay calm folks," she heard one of the men in suits say. "We'll get this all handled and then resume the voting."

Lily was left only with her imagination to wonder what was happening inside. He came out a few moments later, his shirt torn, a dark bruise already forming underneath one eye, and a trickle of blood running out of his mouth. She looked away. She couldn't bear it.

Daddy pursed his lips, grabbed Lily roughly by the hand, and walked inside behind a line of voters. When it was his turn, he quickly cast his ballot. The magical feeling of voting he'd exuded before had vanished, and he deflated like a balloon.

When they came out of City Hall, the colored man was gone and everything was calm. In silence, the two walked to his grocery store. Once inside, Daddy took two caramels out of the candy bin, unwrapped them, popped one in his mouth and held the other out to Lily. He closed his eyes as he chewed, and Lily imagined the sweetness of the candy erasing the bitterness of what they'd seen.

Lily would never forget the look on Daddy's face as they watched that colored man stand up for his right to vote. He wore the same expression tonight at the dinner table. Now that she really thought about it, he'd changed after that day. He'd become more serious, more thoughtful. She wondered if the incident at the store was the last straw for him, that he'd finally broken down. And she wondered what it would all mean for their family.

4

HAZEL

Hazel tried to drag out the day as long as possible, not wanting her time with Miss Grace to end. However, things have a nasty habit of coming to an end whether one wants them to or not, and three o'clock seemed to come extra quick. She collected Glory, and then Willie Jr. and Hallie, who ran ahead of the older girls, headed for home, excited to be officially on summer break.

After a bit, Willie Jr. fell back to match Hazel's steps.

"Why so down?" he teased, nudging Hazel with his elbow. "It's the last day of school! You oughta be happy now, we're free!"

"Not me," Hazel reminded him solemnly. "I love school. You know that. I don't wanna clean up after white folks or pick their crops my whole life."

Willie Jr. looked at her, confused. "And how you gonna do that?"

"I dunno. But I got a feeling school's got the answer."

"Whatever you say!" Willie Jr. laughed maniacally and ran

to catch up with Hallie, flapping his arms. Hazel shook her head but grinned.

Glory was quiet and walked next to Hazel with her head hanging low. Hazel knew she was thinking about being old enough now to help her family this summer. Glory would watch the little ones when Miss Essie couldn't and go to work with Mama at the hotel on the other days. Hazel wasn't sure yet what she'd be doing, but she knew she'd find out soon enough.

"You really think school's our way out, Hazel?" Glory asked quietly.

"I do."

"Then I'll go on thinking that, too," Glory said.

Hazel knew how unfair it was that she and Glory had to grow up so fast. The white girls where Ma Maybelle worked had it so easy. They didn't have to learn to cook or clean; Ma Maybelle did it all for them. Hazel had never met the Wagner girls and didn't much care to meet them. When she was younger, she often felt angry that Ma Maybelle had to leave them to go care for someone else's children. Why couldn't their mother do it? Why couldn't Ma stay with Hazel and her siblings? Now that she was older, she understood that work was a reality of life. That money was needed to survive, however little of it Ma and Mama and Papa brought home for all their hard work. Understanding it didn't erase her anger, though.

Hazel saw the world through the lens of a few facts she knew to be true: White folk separated themselves from colored folk. In fact, white folk felt so strongly about the separation that they wrote actual laws about it. White folk thought they were better than colored folk, and white folk felt free to make life miserable for colored folk. Even in hard times, white folk had it better than their colored neighbors. She couldn't quite wrap her mind around the injustice of it all, but it was all she knew.

When she pushed open the screen door, Hazel found Ma

Maybelle sitting at the kitchen table. Hazel froze. She never came home this early. Had she been fired? Was she sick? Did something happen to Mama or Papa or one of the little ones? All the worst possible things flew through Hazel's mind. She barely had time to realize that Ma Maybelle's face wore a sweet but tired smile.

"Afternoon y'all," she said. She must have seen the look of concern on Hazel's face, because she quickly added, "Lawd, child, don't you go worrying so much. Everything's alright. The Mister and Missus needed some private family time so I came home a little early's all. Help me with supper?"

Hazel let out a breath and nodded. At the mention of help, the younger children fled. "I can do it, Ma, just keep me company and put your feet up, 'kay?"

Hazel was mixing dough and frying up sausage when Ma Maybelle said, "Since Glory'll be working with your mama over at the hotel this summer, whaddya say about coming over to the Wagners' home with me? Missus Wagner thinks she's gonna have some luncheons and that I'll need help with the cooking and cleaning. I think she knows I'm getting old. I told her, 'Missus Wagner, ain't nobody cook as good as me in this whole county, 'cept for maybe Hazel Clementine, my grandbaby.' And Missus Wagner said, 'Well Maybelle, bring her Monday, we'll give it a try.'"

Hazel's brow creased, and Ma sat patiently as she worked through her feelings. On the one hand, she'd never spent time with white folk up close, and the thought made her nervous. But on the other, to get to spend time every day with Ma Maybelle, well, that was something.

She smiled. "Of course, Ma. I'd love to."

"You know," Ma said, "I taught Miss Lily, the youngest Wagner girl, to make those biscuits too. She's almost got 'em as good as you make 'em."

Hazel looked up, surprised. Ma had never really talked about the Wagner girls before, and the thought of Ma spending time to teach another little girl her way around the kitchen made Hazel instantly envious. Her response came out sounding harder than she meant it to. "But why'd she need to know? She'll just grow up and get help like her folks did."

"Now, Hazel. It is my firm belief that every grown person needs to know how to make theirself a good biscuit. And that's that."

Papa came home that night, tired and rundown. His bad knee was bothering him and Hazel knew, so was his arm—what was left of it anyway. Still, he wore a smile for his family, especially the boys who had run outside to greet him. Hazel had cooked up a feast for his homecoming, and as they ate, they overwhelmed him with stories of the neighborhood and school and church. As usual, he took turns sitting with each of his children, talking to them about their week. When it was Hazel's turn, she sat as close to him as she could get, breathing in his fresh-out-of-the-shower scent, one she associated with strength and shelter.

"How was your last day of school, Hazel-girl?"

"It was okay," she said. "But I'll miss it for the summer."

"I know you will, but it'll go fast. I'm proud of you, girl. You my smartest one. Don't tell the others I said so," he told her, his voice low, his tired grin spread across both cheeks.

After the younger ones were asleep, Hazel heard Mama and Papa talking with Ma Maybelle about her helping out at the Wagner house.

"Is it safe? I heard the store got messed up good," Papa said.

"Oh, that? Mr. Wagner just tired of making us folks go through the back, that's all," Ma answered him.

"Well, that man's either real brave or real stupid, Ma," Mama added.

"That's right, Estelle. I don't want her near no white folk, Ma. She don't need to see all that."

"She ain't a child no more, Willie."

"But those girls'll treat her like she's nothing. I can't have that for my girl, not Hazel. She gonna go places."

Hazel grinned at this.

Mama interjected. "Ma knows what she's doing, Willie."

"Sure do. I don't need her help but a couple'a hours a day. Then she can do as she pleases. And besides, I got a feeling her and Miss Lily'll be good for each other."

This statement surprised Hazel. Besides the brief moment earlier, Ma hadn't spoken much about Lily, but surely she couldn't be suggesting that Hazel would get to know her? Like a friend? That, Hazel knew, was absolutely unheard of in Mayfield. The very idea made her stomach twist and turn.

Mama was quiet, but Hazel imagined her nodding her head thoughtfully and giving Papa that look of hers. When she spoke, Hazel hardly heard her words. "Hazel deserves to have a little fun. She spent mosta her childhood running after the young'uns. She ain't had time to be a child. Ma can give her some of that time back."

Before she heard anything else, Hazel crept into her room and snuggled in next to Glory, glad to have her family all under one roof. The bright light of a full moon came in through the window, so she picked up her beautiful new book and read the first chapter, smiling the whole time, thinking of Miss Grace picking it out especially for her.

As she read, Hazel's heart fluttered with a familiar feeling. There was something special about starting a new book: so much potential, a story yet to be told, characters yet to be loved. Hazel tended to read the beginnings of books much slower than she did the middles and the ends. She liked to soak up the beginnings, get a feel for the setting, become friends with the characters.

After reading for a bit, she pulled her notebook out of her bag and wrote a new entry.

Dear Journal,

Miss Grace gave me my very own copy of The Hundred Dresses *today and so far, it's really good. There are two best friends, Maddie and Peggy, about my age. They live in a small town and go to a small school like mine. There's also another girl, Wanda, and she's missing from school. It doesn't seem like Peggy and Maddie even notice she's not there. It got me thinking; would anyone notice if I wasn't at school? Also, where's Wanda? Miss Grace said she's the hero of the story, but I can't see it yet. The book says the girls wait for her in the mornings to "have some fun with her." Those words give me a bad feeling in my belly, like it would not be fun at all for Wanda.*

Until next time,

Hazel

5

LILY

At breakfast the next morning, Mother looked at the girls and said, "I have something to tell you."

Lily stiffened. In her experience, nothing good came after those words. Last time Mother had spoke them, their grandmother in Georgia had fallen ill and did not live through the week. And just last night, Beau had said them when he told Lily they couldn't be friends anymore. So, Lily was not fond of hearing that something "had to be told."

"Girls, your father and I have discussed ways to help the store, in light of... the sign issue... and we would like for you to take delivery shifts this summer. We have a nice bike that you can share, and I expect there to be no complaining. Folks won't want to pass up free grocery delivery, especially in this heat, and hopefully we won't lose many customers. Besides, it's high time you learned the value of hard work."

June scowled but didn't argue, perhaps sensing the seriousness in Mother's voice. June was seventeen and had always been the wisest and most restrained of the sisters. Marianne opened her mouth like she might protest, but seemed to reconsider and instead asked, "Will we get paid?"

"No, you will not. Daddy's store is the reason you have food on this table every day and a roof over your head, so you will pitch in because the store is our family's responsibility."

Marianne pouted and looked away. Lily wasn't exactly excited, but she figured with Beau acting like he was, all she'd have to do this summer was read anyway. Maybe she really would win that contest, and without Beau at that. Or maybe she'd meet someone new, make a new friend. Mayfield was small, but there had to be people she didn't know.

"Also," —*there was more?*— Mother continued, "Maybelle will bring her granddaughter, Hazel, with her this summer. She is getting older and thinks it's time to teach Hazel how to keep a household. Hazel can already cook all of Maybelle's best dishes. You know Maybelle has all those mouths to feed, and we'll pay Hazel a small amount for helping out."

"So, wait." Marianne stuck her lip out even further. "We're gonna pay some little colored girl to work in our house but Daddy's not gonna pay his own daughters for working for him? To beg for customers after a choice *he* made all by himself? This is *so* unfair, Mother!"

Mother turned on her and said, without smiling, "Marianne, you listen to me. Maybelle's been working for this family since before you were born, and not once has she asked us for a thing. Your daddy feels very strongly that this is the Christian thing to do. His mind will not be changed, nor will mine. I will not entertain another word on the matter. Do you understand me?"

Marianne pursed her lips. "Yes ma'am." June just nodded.

"How old is Hazel?" Lily asked, hesitantly. She hadn't heard Mother speak that sternly in a long while, so Lily felt the significance of her words and wanted to tread carefully. She felt like Marianne was being quite obnoxious and spoiled about it all, but did she have a point?

"She's twelve, just like you, Lily, and in fact, I'd really like you to be here when she starts on Monday. Show her around, make her feel welcome."

"Yes ma'am." Deep down, she wasn't sure how she felt about the news. Lily loved Maybelle. What would having another girl in the house be like?

Marianne must've seen the look on Lily's face because she pounced. "What's the matter, Lily? Are you jealous? Of the little colored girl? Because now she'll be Maybelle's favorite?"

"That's quite enough," Mother scolded. "Now get the rest of the table cleared, Marianne."

"Yes, Mother," Marianne responded, but she stuck her tongue out at Lily when she stood up so Mother couldn't see.

Marianne's words stung, but they had made her think. Was she jealous? She knew that Maybelle had a bunch of grandchildren at home, but she'd never given them much thought because here, Maybelle was Lily's, and Lily wanted to keep her all to herself. She hoped that Maybelle would still tell her stories and let her help in the kitchen. If not, it would feel like her two best friends in the world were both gone.

As soon as breakfast was over, Lily headed for the Mayfield Public Library. Her desire to win the reading contest had been further fueled by Beau's nighttime visit. If she wasn't going to have fun adventures with him all summer, well then, she'd just read and read. She'd show him. And dumb old Beulah May. Now she had two people to beat.

Lily hadn't been to the library since she was younger, a child clinging to Mother's hand, but now, a new appreciation for the old building swelled in her chest. There was something familiar in the white columns that framed the steps against the deep red brick. The big live oaks lining the walkway looked like they were ushering her to the door. The instant she stepped inside, the glorious smells of dust and bindings of old books greeted her.

The first thing she spotted was the large portrait of Andrew Carnegie. Lily knew it was because of him and his money that Mayfield had been the first town in the county to get a library. Andrew Carnegie looked down at Lily in approval, as if there were no grander use of one's time than reading a good book. She almost rolled her eyes, but then remembered she was on a mission.

Walking past tall stacks of books that created a maze, she went to the children's section, full of shorter bookshelves and a few comfortable arm chairs for reading. Lily smiled when she saw some of her favorite picture books, those she'd loved but outgrown, sitting atop the shelves, waiting for the right child to pick them up. How had she forgotten how much she'd loved to read?

She wandered around for bit, not even knowing where to start. She typically only read what her teacher assigned; she wasn't even sure what she'd say if someone asked her what she liked to read. After browsing a while, she chose a few books and carried them to the desk where Miss Nora busily filled out catalog cards and organized what looked like a whole stack of new books. The sight excited Lily.

"Well if it isn't Miss Lily Wagner! I'm so glad you came in today. It's sure been a while."

"Hello, Miss Nora. I'm here to get started on the reading contest. I'm going to read all summer!"

"Well, good for you! Let's see what you have here." Miss Nora worked her way through Lily's pile, occasionally commenting on one of the books. "I just know you'll love this one." Or, "This is a really special story."

When she got the end of Lily's stack, she asked, "Can I offer one more suggestion?"

Lily shrugged. "Sure."

Miss Nora handed her a brand-new book with bright colors on the front.

"*The Hundred Dresses?*" Lily asked. "I don't even like dresses. Are you sure this is for me?"

"Oh, yes," Miss Nora said. "It's not just about dresses, you'll see. Give it a try for me, okay? You can bring it back if you find you don't like it."

"Okay. Thank you!"

Miss Nora stamped the due date in the books and pushed the stack over to Lily. "Come back when you're finished with these, and we can chat about them so they'll count for the contest. See, I've already made up the ledger to track everyone's progress!"

She handed Lily a book and flipped to a page that showed a chart. The first column was a list of names, followed by a lot of little boxes to check off the books they read one by one. Lily couldn't wait to get her first checkmark. She grabbed her books, waved to Miss Nora, and ran out the door.

On her way down the steps, she ran smack into Beau, who looked startled but relieved to see her.

"Hey, Lil. Sorry 'bout last night."

She just stared at him. How dare he speak to her?

"C'mon," he said. "Let's go to the creek this afternoon. I got lotsa worms. We could go fish, you and me."

Without one word, Lily marched right past Beau with her nose in the air. She knew she'd probably forgive him eventually, but for now she'd make him squirm. Even though she didn't turn around, she knew Beau was standing there watching her go, his mouth wide open, frozen to his spot.

And she found she didn't much care.

"Now, Hazel," Ma Maybelle said as they took their seats in the back of the bus that took them to the white part of town, "let me tell you 'bout the Wagners. I know I ain't said much 'bout them before, but seeing as you'll be working for 'em, I guess I need to tell you some."

Hazel looked up into her dark brown eyes, recognizing the golden flecks that she saw in her own.

"Mr. Wagner's a good man. He always make sure we got food on the table. And Missus Wagner, she's firm, but a nice lady. She ain't home much, always out volunteering or something. Just stay outta her way and don't get underfoot and you'll be fine. Miss June is serious and don't say much, and Miss Marianne's a silly, spoiled girl. She'll probably ignore you, which is fine. But Miss Lily is spunky, and she laughs at my stories." Hazel's envy flared again but softened when she saw Ma Maybelle's smile.

"Ma, why you gotta call them all 'Miss'? You're older than them and they aren't royalty."

"No, they ain't, but it's a sign of respect."

"Just 'cause they're white?" Hazel wondered.

Ma Maybelle looked out the window and sighed. "It's 'cause we ain't they friends, we they employees. We gotta keep this job. They good people, but you still gotta act right."

Hazel nodded, and they got up to exit the bus.

HAZEL CLUNG to Ma Maybelle's hand as they walked up the front steps of the Wagner house. Three sturdy-looking rocking chairs sat on the porch next to a swinging bench covered with pillows. White pillars framed the steps and extended up to the second-floor balcony. The house looked like someone had recently whitewashed it. It was strange that Ma spent six whole days a week here and Hazel had never seen it before. She had, of course, daydreamed about what it might be like: grand entryway, polished marble floors, ornate furniture, porcelain statuettes everywhere, all ideas from the books she'd read. In reality, the Wagner house wasn't huge, but it was certainly larger than Hazel's, and she was curious to see the inside.

A girl with curly red hair and freckles dotting her cheeks opened the door and greeted them with a genuine smile. Hazel's stomach dropped. She'd seen this girl before, years ago. She'd recognize that red hair anywhere.

"Hello, I'm Lily," she said nervously, biting her lip, but showing no sign of recognizing Hazel. Hazel frowned. What did she have to be nervous about?

"Uh, hi, Miss Lily. I'm Hazel," she replied.

But Lily said, "Oh, please, Hazel, just call me Lily."

Hazel's cheeks burned, and she looked down at her feet. She wondered if the girl had ever told Ma to call her "just Lily."

"Miss Lily, why you up this early? It's summer! Don't you know how to have a vacation?" Ma Maybelle teased her.

Lily tucked a bright red ringlet behind her ear. "Aw Maybelle, it's way too hot to sleep."

"Oh, yes ma'am, it is!"

Inside, Hazel took a good look around. Although the front of the house appeared grand, the inside was simple. The furniture was clean and modest. Nothing looked too expensive like she had expected. And thankfully, they did not seem the type of people who collected little things that just sat there to be dusted.

Hazel had a hard time keeping her mouth from dropping open when Lily walked them into the kitchen. Tall white cabinets lined every wall and a large green island sat in the middle, waiting for experienced hands to work their culinary magic on it. The floor-to-ceiling windows let in the morning light. It was a cheerful room. At home, their kitchen was so small it was difficult to cook a decent meal. But this kitchen was amazing, unlike anything Hazel had ever seen.

Lily left them alone, assured that Ma Maybelle could show Hazel the rest of the house, and they got down to business.

"First thing I do is clean the house, start the morning off with a clean slate. Cleaning will be your job now so I can rest my old knees and focus on the meals, but I'll have you help with the baking and sweets. Mr. Wagner love his sweets. The girls are pretty tidy, and it doesn't take too long to finish. Then I want you to go on and have some fun, you hear? Get in some mischief. Not too much, now."

Hazel smiled as she walked into the dining room and Ma continued, "Like every self-respecting Southern white lady, Missus Wagner has fancy silver to polish and china to care for, but not every day. Then there's just the regular ol' dusting and cleaning windows and sweeping and mopping."

She showed Hazel where the cleaning supplies were, and she got to work. By mid-morning, Hazel had worked her way through the main floor and the downstairs and upstairs bathrooms. Ma had kept the house so clean it was easy work. She tentatively stepped into the girls' hallway, thankful they weren't home. Hazel looked around. She guessed the first room she entered was Miss June's. Loose papers lay scattered on the bed—not the floor, at least—covered in complicated mathematical equations. Large textbooks sat on a short wooden dresser, and another stack of books were neatly piled up by the bed. Hazel cleaned it quickly and moved on.

The other bedroom was huge. How nice it would be to have a room that size to share with her brothers and sisters! The matching twin beds looked like princess beds: four spindles on each, topped with round balls, handmade wedding-ring patterned quilts, soft pillows. Hazel could already tell who lived on which side. Miss Marianne's side was littered with clothes that Hazel picked up and placed gingerly on the unmade bed with her thumb and forefinger. Next to the bed was a simple mirrored vanity cluttered with curlers and a collection of brightly colored lipsticks.

Miss Lily's side was tidier. Her bed was made, and a bookshelf stood between it and the door. It was low enough to serve as a nightstand and a delicate pink lamp sat on top, along with a stack of books. Each one had a sticker on the front that read "Mayfield Public Library" which made Hazel's heart clench. She wasn't allowed in the public library. Her fingers itched at the sight of all those books. She knew it wasn't right to go through Miss Lily's things, but she looked at the book covers anyway, careful to put them back exactly as she had found them.

It was still before noon when Hazel had finished cleaning, so Ma Maybelle shooed her out the door. She took the exact route they had taken this morning, only this time in reverse, and rather than catching the bus, Hazel decided to walk instead. It wasn't all that much farther, and Hazel liked to feel the blood pumping through her veins, even if it was ungodly hot outside. Once she had crossed over into the colored side of town, she felt relief, like she could breathe again. The knot that had wound its way around her insides slowly unraveled, and she knew right where to go. Settling down in the shade of her favorite oak, she read more of *The Hundred Dresses* and then the last entry she had written before adding another to her notebook.

Dear Journal,

Now I know why they want to "have fun" with Wanda. Trying to fit in with the girls one day, Wanda told Peggy and Maddie that she had a hundred dresses "all lined up in her closet." Peggy and Maddie know that Wanda lives on the poor side of town, and they know it's impossible for her to have all those dresses. Besides, she always wears the same dress to school, and they think she is strange. So they tease Wanda and play the "dresses game" every day. They are bullies, plain and simple. I don't know if poor Wanda even knows they're being hateful. Peggy and Maddie got all the girls in their class in on it, and they only noticed Wanda was gone because they didn't get to tease her one day. But Maddie knows what they're doing is wrong, and it's awful she won't stand up to Peggy. I almost hope Wanda doesn't come back, for her own sake.

Until next time,
Hazel

WHEN THE SUN began to hang a little lower in the sky, Hazel got up and walked back to the Wagners', hoping to help Ma finish up any last-minute work and then make the journey home together. She had a feeling that their travels to and from home would be the highlight of her summer. Ma told the best stories and taught Hazel so many things about life, about real life. Her experience and wisdom were unmatched in Hazel's eyes, and she vowed not to let the summer pass by idly or let any story go unheard.

7

LILY

After leaving Maybelle and Hazel in the kitchen, Lily found a piece of salt-water taffy and a note with her name on it, in Daddy's handwriting.

Lily Jo,
As soon as you're done with breakfast, come on down to the store. I'll have a delivery ready for you when you get there.
Love, Daddy

By the time Lily got to Wagner's Market, beads of sweat dripped down into her eyes. It was already over a hundred degrees. She walked into the back of the store, smiling when she spotted the familiar "Where Friends Meet for Meat!" sign over the deli counter. She walked past wooden barrels full of boiled peanuts and pickled pig's feet and breathed in her favorite scent: fresh ground coffee. Marty Phillips had already packed up the grocery order for her. Sixteen and handsome, Marty was Daddy's best stock boy. Marty spotted Lily and, rather like a big brother, clapped her on the back.

"Good morning, Miss Lily. I hope your chariot's in good working order, I got a big order for you. It's for Mrs. Shaw in the boarding house. And it's a hot one out there."

"Mrs. Sh...Shaw?"

"Don't believe everything you hear, Lily. She's a nice lady. And those girls need to eat, right?"

Lily shrugged and wiped the sweat off her forehead for the umpteenth time. "I guess?"

Marty noticed. "Hey, I got a secret spot for cooling off, wanna see?" he whispered and held out his hand. Not one to be picky, Lily took it and followed him right into the meat cooler.

A burst of freezing air rushed at her as they stepped inside, and she grinned at Marty. Lily had never been in the freezer before, despite the fact that she'd practically grown up in the store. The giant hunks of hanging meat turned her stomach though, so she closed her eyes and let the frigid air wash over her. Before long, they got too cold, something Lily had thought impossible during a South Carolina summer, and Marty opened the door so they could step back into the stuffy stock room. He gave Lily the house number for Mrs. Shaw and then loaded the groceries into the basket on the front of her bicycle.

Mrs. Shaw lived in a big house, one block off of Main Street, where Lily knew she ran a boarding house for young ladies. Lily had heard the worst of the rumors about Mrs. Shaw, that she lured children into her home so she could eat them—a modern-day Hansel and Gretel witch—that she had something sinister to do with her husband's death, that the house was haunted by his ghost. Mrs. Shaw was a favorite topic of the ladies of Mayfield, since she often turned down invitations to bridge luncheons and afternoon tea. Lily couldn't remember actually ever seeing the woman, but she'd been past the house enough to associate it with everything she'd heard, and she always found herself speeding up to get by it quickly.

Now, the large house loomed over Lily like a cross old man, and the steps groaned as she climbed them. Her hands shook as she gently grabbed the large brass knocker and rapped three times. A tall, stern-looking woman opened the door and peered down her nose at Lily. Her dark hair was pulled back in a neat bun, so tight it looked uncomfortable. The old-fashioned black taffeta dress she wore made her look like she was in mourning, although Lily knew that it had been several years since Mr. Shaw had passed on. With a shiver, images of an old man's ghost, pale as a sheet, ran through her mind without her permission, and Lily wondered how the woman in front of her could stand that dress in this heat. Mrs. Shaw's thin lips wore a frown, one that looked to be permanent and made her appear much older than her thirty-something years.

"Can I help you, young lady? I do hope you're not selling anything, I'm very busy."

"I... I... I'm Lily Wagner? From Wagner's Market? I have your groceries?" Lily stammered.

"Oh yes, yes, come in, then."

Mrs. Shaw left the door open, and Lily went back to the bike to grab the groceries. There were a lot of heavy bags, and Lily struggled to get up the steps and into the house. Mrs. Shaw walked down the hall to the large kitchen where Lily could smell lunch cooking on the stove. The phone rang, and Mrs. Shaw answered it. Unsure of what to do, Lily looked around and decided to set the grocery bags on an ornate table that sat in the window nook.

Relieved to have the bags out of her hands, Lily turned around just in time to see a pan on the stove burst into flames.

"Oh, Mrs. Shaw!" Lily cried out.

Mrs. Shaw didn't even look at Lily as she hissed, "Don't interrupt me girl, I'm on the phone!"

"But Mrs. Shaw, your stove! It's on *fire!*"

That got her attention, and Mrs. Shaw dropped the phone and ran to the stove. She turned off the burners and put a lid on the flaming pan.

Mrs. Shaw was still out of breath as she counted out the cash she owed Daddy for the groceries. She added an extra nickel and said, "For saving us all from burning up, Miss Wagner. Now get on, I have work to do. And next time, do try to come at a better time, not smack in the middle of lunch."

"Yes'm," Lily mumbled and headed back to her bike. She shuddered—something about the woman made Lily uneasy, but she couldn't tell if it was her surliness or all the rumors she'd heard over the years. Lily would be just fine if there wasn't a "next time."

At home that afternoon, Lily sat on the porch swing and began reading *The Hundred Dresses*, the book Miss Nora had picked out for her. She rolled her eyes again at the title, but opened it anyway. Soon, she found herself getting completely lost in the story, wanting to forget the incident with Mrs. Shaw. When she heard the Adams's front door open, she glanced over at their porch. But it wasn't Beau who'd opened the door; it was his pa, and he didn't even look in Lily's direction. When she turned her attention back to her own porch, something under the rocking chair next to the front door caught her eye. She got out of the swing and walked over, and then picked up what looked like a notebook. It bore Hazel's name. Making sure she was alone, Lily opened it and read the last few entries before the latest one.

Dear Journal,

  Maddie is just making me mad. She won't stand up to Peggy to make her stop teasing Wanda. The more I read, the more I think Wanda probably doesn't know what they are really doing. And the more I am convinced that it would be better if she never came back. I wonder if she even speaks English that well. Her last name, Petronski, is strange, not like the other kids. Also, Boggins Heights, where Wanda lives, sounds a little like the colored side of Mayfield to me, where white folks don't feel safe and where everything is older and more worn down.

  Until next time,
  Hazel

AT FIRST, Lily was too stunned to understand what she'd read. She couldn't believe Hazel was reading the very same book she was. And, she'd never heard of someone writing about the books they were reading. Not even her teachers made them do that until they finished a book and had to do a dumb book report. But she was completely enthralled with Hazel's thoughts. She'd had some of the same thoughts as she read along, but they hadn't stuck to her mind until she read Hazel's words.

Lily leaned back on her swing and smiled, hugging the notebook to her chest. So Hazel liked books, too! If reading was going to be Lily's new pastime, could Hazel perhaps be the new friend Lily had been longing for?

Her happiness quickly faded, though, when she remembered that there would be consequences from being friends with the colored help. She realized that, although her parents might not mind, out in town it would be frowned upon. Beau and his pa had made that abundantly clear.

After all, things were separate in Mayfield. Colored folks

had their own bathrooms and doctor's offices and water foun-
tains and restaurants. They lived in a separate part of town,
much like the fictional Boggins Heights, now that Lily thought
about it. They went to separate schools and had their own
churches. In fact, the only places colored and white folks inter-
mingled were in stores like her daddy's. And even there, people
stayed as separate as they could.

Until she read Hazel's journal, she'd never really thought
about how it was to be on the other side. Separation was
normal, all she'd ever known. She'd never thought to question
it. And even though the way Wanda was being treated in her
book had started to bother her, she couldn't quite put her finger
on just why.

She could tell that Hazel understood this in a way she
didn't.

———

An hour later when Hazel and Maybelle left for the evening,
Lily made sure to be sitting in the rocker right by the front door.
And she made sure to be reading *The Hundred Dresses*, its
colorful cover displayed for all to see.

The door opened and Lily saw Hazel pause ever-so-slightly
when she saw the book. But she clenched her jaw and looked
ahead. When Lily reached out and lightly touched her arm,
Hazel recoiled.

"I think you dropped this," Lily said, like it was no big deal.
Hazel looked at her then, her eyes wide, searching Lily's face.
Maybelle nudged Hazel forward, as if to unstick her, and Hazel
grabbed the journal, setting her gaze firmly to the street ahead.

"Thank you, Miss Lily." Hazel didn't look back, but
Maybelle gave Lily a knowing sort of smile and the two walked
off together.

8

HAZEL

While Mama fixed beans with ham and cornbread for supper, the other children peppered Hazel with questions. She knew it was natural for them to be curious. None of them had ever been in a white family's house either. Hazel described the house and the furniture just enough to satisfy them, but she also kept some details to herself. She didn't tell them about Lily finding her journal. She didn't tell them about looking through Lily's books or the way her heart had raced when she'd seen *The Hundred Dresses* in Lily's hand.

Hazel must have dropped the journal in her haste to get back to help Ma finish the day. Now she wondered if Lily had read it, but as she wanted to keep it away from Willie Jr.'s eyes and inevitable teasing, she made herself wait until later to open it and had to settle for her own worries about it instead. What happened next all depended on the kind of girl Lily was. She seemed nice enough, but Hazel hadn't had enough time to see for herself.

Miss Grace had taught them that there was a time, in the not-so-distant past, when white folk passed laws against teaching colored folk to read and write, especially during the time of slavery, the idea being that educated slaves would be able to figure out how to escape or start questioning the institution of slavery. Even now, Hazel knew there were still white folk who felt that way, since colored children weren't allowed in the library or in their schools.

After dinner, Hazel grabbed her journal and book and left the house, heading straight for her spot under the oak tree once again. Before she could get back to Maddie and Peggy and Wanda, she opened the journal and was shocked to find another entry, after her last one, in a flowing cursive handwriting she'd never seen before.

Dear Hazel,

I hope it's okay that I write in here. I'm reading The Hundred Dresses, *too, and it seems like you're enjoying it as much as I am. I also hope it's okay that I read what you wrote. I was thinking a lot of the same things you were, and you made me think about some other things I never would have by myself.*

Have you gotten to the part when the contest winners are announced yet? I haven't, but I'm anxious to find out. I think you might be onto something with your thoughts about Boggins Heights. I hadn't considered it until now, as it's just the way Mayfield's always been, but it does seem unfair, doesn't it? I've heard folks say "separate but equal," but are they equal? The other kids act like something's wrong with Wanda just because she lives in Boggins Heights. That doesn't seem very fair.

The other interesting thing is that Maddie is poor, too, but tries to hide it. She's scared of getting treated like Wanda, which makes me think: why'd she go along with the game in

the first place? I wish she'd stand up to Peggy and tell her to
stop the dresses game. I hope you'll write back, but of course
that's up to you.
    Yours sincerely,
    Lily

HAZEL COULDN'T DECIDE how she felt about Lily writing in
her journal. The first thing she felt was anger; how *dare* she
read and then write in Hazel's journal? Would Lily have been
bold enough to do this in one of her white classmate's journals?
The audacity of it all rather shocked Hazel, and it took a few
minutes to compose herself. Her anger then morphed into
worry that Lily had caught her doing something she shouldn't
when she should be working. Would she tell her parents? But
then, as she read it again and again, still in a state of disbelief,
Hazel calmed a bit as she realized that Lily's tone in the letter
felt sincere, like she was talking to a friend.

The thought stopped her, though; could she actually be
friends with Lily? How would that even work? Hazel had never
considered being friends with a white girl, and now the thought
of it equally exhilarated her and scared her to death. She
thought about Wanda, how she bravely kept showing up even
when those girls were so mean, and she decided she could be
brave, too. So she wrote Lily back and made a plan.

That night, she hardly slept. The unbearable heat and her
noisy siblings kept her awake, but her mind also could not let go
of what Lily had written in the journal.

THE NEXT MORNING Hazel left Ma Maybelle in the kitchen to
clean up after the Wagners' breakfast alone, saying she wanted
to get a head start on the rest of the house. All the ladies were

out attending a canned food charity event for the soldiers over-seas, giving Hazel a perfect opportunity to do what she wanted to do.

She tiptoed up the stairs to Lily's room and left the journal right on the nightstand in the middle of the stack of books, hoping Lily would recognize it. Since she had the whole day to clean, Hazel then chose a book from Lily's stack and sat on the floor, her back up against Lily's plush mattress, and she read. And read. And read.

It wasn't until she heard Ma holler, "Hazel! You done?" that she snapped out of it, quickly ran a dust rag over the flat surfaces of the room and went back downstairs. Deeper cleaning could wait until tomorrow.

Mrs. Wagner had invited guests for dinner, the reverend of the Methodist church and his wife. According to Ma, this was because the Wagners were trying to get back in Mayfield's good graces after the incident at the store, which Ma had told Hazel was utterly ridiculous. But they prepared the meal anyhow. Ma Maybelle was busy cooking the truest of Southern feasts: fried chicken, mashed potatoes, and her best creamed corn. Hazel started on a strawberry rhubarb pie for dessert, one she'd been baking since she was tall enough to work at the kitchen counter.

As she mixed the dough for the crust and sliced the fruit, Hazel wondered if Lily would write back. And furthermore, was it even okay for them to be friends?

9

LILY

On her way home from the fundraising event at the church, Lily tried to join the neighborhood baseball game. Life had mostly gone on as normal. Even though the store seemed a little emptier than usual, they still had plenty of customers. And the Wagner girls had made a good show at the church, working hard all day, long past even when their mother had left, showing that they loved Mayfield just as much as anyone else. And right this minute, Mother and Daddy were hosting the minister and his wife for dinner. Marianne had loudly made sure everyone knew about that. She and June had gone home for supper, but Lily had been inside too long, so she went looking for the game she knew happened every night.

There was just one problem: Lily still hadn't spoken to Beau.

Lily was a good ball player, scrappy and competitive. Normally, the boys all begged for her to be on their teams, but as she walked up to them, not one would meet her eye, pretending like she didn't exist.

The street lamps popped on one by one, and the game was

all set up in the street. Spotting Beau on his usual makeshift third base, she marched over and punched him on the arm.

Hard.

"So what? You got all them to be mad at me, too? What's wrong with you, Beaumont?"

Beau stared at her, stunned, and rubbed his arm where she'd hit him. "Aw come on Lil, it wasn't me. I think... they just don't want a girl to play anymore, that's all."

He might as well have slapped her across the face.

Lily opened her mouth to respond, but the boys had all jogged over to where they were standing and she turned just as Dalen Rowe said, "Hey Beau, get that colored-loving daddy's girl off our field! We got a game to play."

Oh, this was so much worse than she'd thought.

She wheeled around to face Beau again. His cheeks reddened and he mumbled, "Okay fine, Lil. But it wasn't me that did it." The next moment, it seemed that a burst of courage made its way up Beau's throat. "C'mon Dalen. Who cares what her daddy did? You know she's the best player we got."

Tom Gordon, whose daddy was Butch, the man with the gun at the store who really started all this business, spoke up. "Best player or not, she can't play. Go on home, now, play with your dollies. Are your dollies colored too? I bet you'd love some little colored baby dollies." He said this last sentence with an obnoxious whine to it, so it sounds more like "whittle cowwerd baby dowwies."

Lily couldn't remember ever being this angry. She yanked the boys' only extra ball out of Tom's hand and ran down the street, trying to hide the tears streaming down her cheeks. She heard them shouting after her, but didn't turn around. Before she was out of their sight, she threw the ball as hard and far as she could.

Unfortunately, she hadn't realized she was standing right in front of the boarding house, and the baseball hit the porch steps with a sickening *thud*. Lily froze. Mrs. Shaw was sitting in a wooden rocker under a single lightbulb, a book in her hand, glasses perched on the end of her nose.

"Miss Wagner, is that you?" Mrs. Shaw asked sharply. Lily nodded, still unable to move, tears still falling down her face. "I don't know what it is you're upset about, young lady, but I better never see you throw anything at my house again. Understand?"

"Ye... Yes'm," Lily managed.

Leaving the ball right where it had landed, Lily walked toward home. She guessed things weren't as back to normal as she thought. Is this how her whole summer was going to go?

When she got home, she went around back to the kitchen door so she wouldn't disturb her parents and Reverend Lucas. Marianne and June were in the kitchen, eating plates of fried chicken and mashed potatoes. Lily's mouth watered as June pushed a plate toward her.

"Shh," Marianne said, putting a finger to her lips, pointing at the door leading to the dining room.

Lily could hear voices, louder than usual for polite company.

"Now see here, Clarke," Reverend Lucas said in the voice he used from the pulpit on Sundays. "I see why you did what you did, but that has to be as far as this goes. Or I can no longer in good faith defend you to the congregation. Actions have consequences."

"But don't you think it's *wrong*, sir? The Bible says 'all tribes and peoples and languages'."

"Don't go quoting the Bible at me, Clarke. I know well what it says. We're not keeping them from God. We are charged with peace, though, and keeping the peace means we keep separate. Best for them folk to stay over there in their place, and us to stay over here in ours."

Daddy must have not had much to say back to that, because it got very quiet until Rebecca, the reverend's wife, cleared her throat and said in a kind but tight voice, "Miriam, this pie is simply *divine*."

The talk then became too quiet for the sisters to hear. Marianne licked the last bit of creamed corn off her fork and said, "Reverend Lucas is right, you know. Mixing things up would just cause rioting and unrest."

Lily looked at June, her mouth wide open in surprise. "And what do you know of rioting and unrest, dear sister?" June asked, the venom in her voice apparent.

Marianne slouched back in her seat and shrugged. "I just know I feel safer over here than I would if they were over here, too."

Lily felt her cheeks get hot. "But," she hissed, trying to whisper because otherwise she was afraid she'd scream it, "what about Maybelle? And Hazel? You can't think they are dangerous!"

"They work here, Lily. You don't know what they're like when they go home. Or what the men over there act like. I know I wouldn't wanna meet one of them on a dark street." Then, like she was bored with the conversation, Marianne put her dishes in the sink and walked out of the kitchen, flipping her hair on the way out.

June looked right at Lily. "Don't listen to her. She's just too dumb to see she's wrong."

THE NEXT MORNING, Lily hopped on her bike and rode to Daddy's store. He gave her a big grin as she walked in, but he was busy helping a customer, so she began to wander the aisles. It was a slow day, and Lily found Marty reshelving items and organizing canned goods.

"Miss Lily, what brings you here on this lovely Monday?"

"Aw, nothing, just bored."

Marty smiled. "Well come on and help then, don't just stand there." He handed Lily two cans of green beans.

"Yuck!" she said, scrunching up her face.

"What?" Marty asked. "You don't like green beans? Who doesn't like green beans?"

"Oh, I do! Just not the canned ones. Maybelle makes the very best green beans, you know. She fries up a fatty piece of bacon and cooks them 'til they're perfect. Not too soggy, not too crunchy."

"Mmm... you're making my mouth water! But I see your point."

"I just think the canned ones are too soft right from the start—"

"—so they can never really recover, right?" Marty finished, completing her thought.

"Exactly!" Lily smiled and, personal feelings aside, added the cans to the top of the stack.

While she worked, she looked around the store. Lily noticed that, of the few people shopping, most were colored women dressed in maids' uniforms. They pushed their carts slowly and smiled briefly at each other as they passed.

She watched Mrs. Johansen, a lady who lived on Lily's street, approach the produce section and look down at a colored maid who was choosing some apples. Mrs. Johansen must have felt the colored woman was taking too long because she made a loud huffing sound and started to tap her foot impatiently.

"Move along now, Negro," Mrs. Johansen snarled. The colored woman looked down and quickly walked away. Lily was close enough to Mrs. Johansen to hear her murmur, "He just had to let them walk in the front, didn't he?" to a woman next to her. "They think they own the place now," came the sharp reply.

Lily felt disoriented; Mrs. Johansen had always been so kind to her, but this was a completely different side of the woman. Ever since she'd read Hazel's journal about *The Hundred Dresses* and the colored side of town, Lily had started to look at Mayfield and its people through new eyes. A little voice inside her head whispered, *but why is it like this?* And it made Lily uncomfortable that she didn't know the answer.

Daddy interrupted her thoughts. "I'm so glad you're here, sweetheart. Mrs. Parrish just called and needs some last-minute things. Here, let me get you a list and you can bag it up and run it over to her."

Lily didn't enjoy the thought of taking groceries to her music teacher's house—how embarrassing—but she got the groceries bagged just the same. At least it wasn't the boarding house.

As soon as she got home after making the delivery, Lily opened up *The Hundred Dresses* and finished the last chapter. It hadn't ended exactly the way she'd hoped, but she supposed things couldn't all be tied up with a nice bow all the time. When she went to look through the other books she'd borrowed from the library, she spotted Hazel's notebook, situated right in the stack like it had always been there. She smiled and opened it, reading Hazel's latest entry.

Dear Lily,

I finished the book tonight. I'm glad Wanda had the last say. I think this is what Miss Grace meant about her being the hero. And I'm glad that Maddie felt bad about what they did. I still have questions though, like did Wanda know that they were bullying her? I almost hope she didn't, because that makes for a happier story. I would love to see all her paintings of the dresses and to know what was really in Peggy's heart. We know what Maddie was thinking, but is it possible that Peggy wouldn't ever change? Do you think people can change that much? I'd like to hope so, but I just don't know. I'm sad now that the book is over. I'm interested in your thoughts on the ending too, but I guess we don't need to write again after that.

    Sincerely,

    Hazel

    P.S. I wish I had another good book to read.

THE POSTSCRIPT LOOKED like it had been written, then erased, then written again, as if Hazel couldn't make up her mind to share this longing with Lily. It warmed Lily's heart that she decided to include it in the end. And then she became determined to find Hazel a book, and a good book at that, so that she could keep reading and they could keep writing back and forth. Lily wasn't ready to be done with that.

10

HAZEL

JULY 1945

T rue to her word, Hazel left early the next morning to tell
Miss Grace she had finished the book. With a promise to
Ma Maybelle that she'd be over at the Wagners' shortly, Hazel
walked over to Miss Grace's house. Hazel knew she'd be there,
doing laundry for some white folks in town, like she did every
summer.

Miss Grace was the type of teacher who told her students
the whole truth about things, even hard things. Hazel remembered the day she brought in a newspaper article from *The
Mayfield Gazette* that published teacher's salaries, including
her own. The white teachers in Mayfield at the Wagner girls'
schools had salaries that were more than double that of Miss
Grace's. Miss Grace had not shown her students this to
complain, rather to show how the newspaper had been
unashamed to publish the numbers. But it did explain why
Miss Grace took on summer work. And, Hazel supposed
quietly to herself, it explained why the textbooks at their school
were always hand-me-downs from the white schools, why their

building was more run down, why their football fields had no bleachers or goal posts.

Miss Grace sat in her small kitchen, and Hazel could see her through the window as she approached the door. She knocked quietly so she wouldn't alarm Miss Grace and heard a cheerful, "Come on in!" so she turned the handle and pushed open the door.

Miss Grace poured Hazel a glass of iced tea and said, "Well, don't keep me waiting, girl! How'd you like the book?"

"I loved it. It was hard to read about the game those mean girls played, but I'm glad at least one of 'em changed her ways by the end," Hazel began.

"Ah yes, our Maddie," Miss Grace said. "I thought you might like her."

"She still made me really mad, not standing up to Peggy," Hazel continued.

"I agree with you there. Unfortunately, sometimes we learn lessons too late. But I like to think that we become better people after we learn them."

"Right," Hazel said. "So it's like the author wanted us to know that even if we can't fix something in the moment, we can always try harder next time?"

"Yes, exactly. Now you're thinking like a true reader. I just knew you'd love the book. But I can see that something's troubling you. Go on, don't chew a hole through your lip. Let's have it." Miss Grace looked Hazel square in the face, not as a challenge, but to show Hazel that she had her teacher's full attention.

"It's just that," Hazel started, "the girls in the book, even as young as they were, already broke into groups by the kids who had money and the ones who didn't. It seems like all folks wanna do is separate everyone. Even our school, our part of Mayfield being separate, our bathrooms, our restaurants. I know it's 'cause white folks think they're better than us. What I don't know is why. They got more money, sure, but there's poor white folks, too. It just seems like folks keep doing things how they've always done them, no questions asked. I got a little jealous of Wanda 'cause she got to go to school with the rest of them, still had the same opportunities."

Hazel stopped, her cheeks reddening at her new-found boldness and passion.

"Ah, yes. And now you're reading like a true scholar, one who questions things about our world, especially the things that feel unfair." Miss Grace looked at Hazel with sad, but proud, eyes. "You're growing on up Hazel, realizing how things are. But I can tell you are growing in exactly the right direction."

Hazel gave her a shy smile. "But Miss Grace, what do we do about it? Just sit here and watch? Let it be? Fight against it?"

"Well now, I believe that knowledge can be one of our best weapons. We learn about how it is. We learn about other people. We learn about how other people have dealt with hard issues before. We learn about ourselves and what's deep down inside us and we learn to drown out the voices of others who think we are less than we are."

The words struck a chord with Hazel. Back in August, she might not have understood them, but now she knew what Miss Grace meant.

"And that's why you became a teacher, right, Miss Grace? To teach us all of this?"

Miss Grace nodded gravely. "You got it, Miss Hazel Clementine, that is it exactly. I teach so that hopefully you children will grow up knowing you're somebody, knowing you're important. And my hope is that after you've learned all you can from me and others, one of you might go out and change the world armed with the strength of your own knowledge."

Hazel let Miss Grace's words swirl around until they found just the spot to rest in her mind.

They sat quietly for a few moments before Hazel remembered the time. "Oh! I'm sorry Miss Grace but I've gotta go. Thanks again for the book. I think I'll give it to Glory to read next."

"The more readers, the better, I always say," Miss Grace replied. "Go on, now, and come back and see me sometime soon you hear? I enjoyed our talk this morning."

"Yes'm, me too!"

Hazel hurried to the bus stop, not wanting to miss the next ride to the white side of town. Now that her attention was turned toward all the injustices around her, she couldn't stop thinking about it. On the bus ride she really saw, perhaps for the first time, how the homes in her neighborhood compared to Lily's. The small houses left something to be desired: paint peeling off cracked wood, roofs visibly patched in mismatched colors, windows stuck open permanently or gone altogether, fences that looked like a slight breeze could blow them down. Everything seemed older and more weathered.

On the walk from the bus stop to the Wagners', Hazel's mind drifted to Lily. One of the most unfair things, in Hazel's mind, was the unspoken rule that white and colored children did not become friends. Lily had written to her, taken a chance, opened the door. Was she different? Maybe Hazel could start fighting against that unfairness now, in her own small way, by being a real friend to Lily.

The thought put a small smile on Hazel's face, and she skipped happily up the Wagners' lawn. She couldn't wait to see if Lily had left a note in the journal. But then she spotted Lily rocking on the porch swing with a new book in her hands, without a care in the world, and just like that, Hazel's good mood disappeared. Bitterness and jealousy flowed through her.

How Hazel would love to spend an afternoon reading, no cleaning to do or meals to cook.

No, Hazel decided, they were too different to be friends. She hung her head low and mumbled a tight-lipped, "Hello, Miss Lily," before climbing the steps and walking in to find Ma Maybelle.

11

LILY

E arlier that day, Daddy had called the house and told Lily that Mrs. Shaw needed her groceries delivered again. She groaned. When she told Daddy about the almost-fire, Lily was annoyed that he'd thrown back his head and laughed instead of showing real concern for her safety.

"Please, Daddy, make one of the other girls take it. That woman is awful scary," she begged.

"No can do, Lily Jo. They are nowhere to be found. It's gonna have to be you, darlin'."

So Lily, wanting to please her father, took the groceries and was soon on her way.

LILY RAPPED on the front door of the boarding house, whispering a quiet prayer that Mrs. Shaw wouldn't be cooking or that maybe she wouldn't even be home. Luckily, one of the boarding girls opened the door with a smile. Seeing the groceries, she offered to help Lily bring them in. Talking over her shoulder, she said, "Mrs. Shaw's in the library. Let's take this food to the kitchen and then I'll walk you back there, okay? I'm Rose, by the way."

"Lily. Pleased to meet you, ma'am."

"Stop that this instant. I'm no ma'am," Rose replied with a wink.

"So, Mrs. Shaw has a library? Right in this very house?" Lily asked, curious.

"Oh yes. It's wonderful. One of the reasons I enjoy living here. Do you like to read?"

Lily smiled and instantly felt like she was with a kindred spirit. "I'm liking it more lately. If you can believe it, I kind of forgot how much I loved books until just this summer. In fact, there's a summer reading contest for my school, and I aim to win."

"That's fantastic!" Rose pulled canned vegetables and bread out of the grocery bags and put them away. "What do you like to read?"

"I just finished a new book called *The Hundred Dresses*. It was delightful."

"That sounds lovely!" Rose said as she put away the last of the groceries.

With a sudden stroke of courage, Lily blurted out, "So, what's Mrs. Shaw like? She scares me a bit."

Rose giggled, then lowered her voice to an audible whisper. "She has a prickly exterior, which helps her keep control around here. I think she's got a good, kind heart, but likes to keep to herself, so maybe she's a little misunderstood around town." She continued, louder this time, "Let's go find her so she can pay for the groceries."

Rose led Lily down a dark corridor to a brightly lit room with white double French doors and then said, "Oh, heavens! Look at the time! I must get going. I have a study group in ten minutes! Go on, see the library for yourself. Mrs. Shaw will be so happy to know you are a reader! Nice to meet you, Lily!" she shouted as she ran up the stairs.

Lily peered curiously through the windowed doors and saw a most magnificent sight: white floor-to-ceiling bookshelves covered all three interior walls, minus a cut-out for the bright window with a view of the lush garden in the back. A large wooden rolling ladder stood against one of the shelves.

A voice interrupted Lily's admiration. "Well come in, then. Lily is it, Miss Wagner?"

"Yes ma'am." Lily took a deep breath as she entered the beautiful room. She found Mrs. Shaw in a comfortable-looking armchair. Her dark hair fell in a long braid down the front of her shoulder. She wore a pale green dress, one that brightened her features and gave color to her cheeks. A novel called *Wuthering Heights* sat on her lap. Although Lily hadn't read it, she knew the book was a classic. Strangely, seeing Mrs. Shaw in her library softened Lily's impression of the woman. She looked more relaxed than the first times they had met, not as stern and serious.

Wringing her hands, Lily stammered, "I... I'm sorry about the baseball."

"Thank you, but it's quite alright. There was no real harm done."

"This is a lovely room, Mrs. Shaw," Lily said, relaxing a little.

Mrs. Shaw closed her novel and smiled. Lily hadn't seen it before, but Mrs. Shaw had a rather pretty smile.

"Why thank you, I'm quite proud of it. I like to make sure the girls all have access to great literature. It's very important to their education, you see."

"Yes, ma'am," Lily replied, still unsure of how to speak to the imposing woman.

"I heard your conversation in the hallway with Rose and I'm delighted to hear that you love to read. Please feel free to borrow any book you like, just let me know what you take."

Lily's eyes grew wide. "That would be wonderful, Mrs. Shaw," she whispered, amazed at the offer. "Thank you ever so kindly. In fact, I need a new book to read. I just finished one."

"I have just the thing for a girl your age!" Mrs. Shaw got up and strode over to the shelf to the right of the window. After drumming her fingers along the spines, she chose a book, an older one, well-worn with a leather cover. "Might I suggest this one? It's a favorite of mine."

Lily took the book gingerly, as if Mrs. Shaw had handed her a priceless heirloom. The cover was a deep green color and the title read, *Anne of Green Gables* by Lucy Maude Montgomery.

"The main character, Anne, with an 'E' as she says, has red hair just like yours and she's a real spitfire. I know you'll love it. Go on, take it home. Bring it on back when you're through and make sure to tell me how you liked it."

Lily was speechless. A woman she had been terrified of just a few short hours ago was now lending her a book? And with a smile? She promised to take care of the book, and gave Mrs. Shaw an enthusiastic, "Thank you!" before collecting the grocery fee and heading out the door.

LILY RODE her bike to the library, where she told Miss Nora all about *The Hundred Dresses*. While Miss Nora recorded the book on the chart in her ledger, Lily noticed that Beulah May already had two marks by her name. This made Lily want to hurry home to read *Anne of Green Gables* and a few others, too. However, on her way inside, she had spotted something and before she left, had a thought and turned back, asking Miss

Nora where she could find *Anne* in the library. Miss Nora, as
always, knew exactly upon which shelf it sat. Lily quickly
checked it out, stuffed it in her bag, and raced home.

Hazel found her ten minutes later, on the porch swing,
book in hand. Lily could see that something was bothering
Hazel, but she couldn't imagine what it would be. After all,
besides that first day and the letters in the notebook, the two
girls hadn't shared any real conversations. When the front door
slammed behind her, Lily decided that something was defi-
nitely wrong, so she hopped up and followed her inside.

Hazel was dusting the living room and doing all she could
to avoid eye contact with Lily. Lily opened her mouth to ask if
she was all right, but then snapped it shut when Hazel said,
rather tersely, "Excuse me, Miss Lily," to get to the bookshelf
behind her. So Lily wandered into the kitchen instead, pleased
to find Maybelle cooking the chocolate pudding that would
need to cool before dinner. Chocolate pudding was Lily's
favorite.

"Hi, Maybelle," Lily started out. "Is Hazel okay? She
seemed a little... frazzled just now."

Maybelle sighed a deep sigh, the kind that leaves both lungs
empty. She paused for a moment as if she was considering
whether or not to share anything with Lily and then softened.

"Here, Sugar, you stir the pudding. Make sure to get out all
them lumps." Maybelle handed Lily the whisk and moved to
the sink to rinse some catfish for supper.

"As for Hazel, she's alright, just growing on up like you,
realizing things ain't as good as she'd like them to be, that's all."

"Well, Maybelle, to tell you the God's honest truth, I've
been thinking a lot about things, too. Especially about how
things in Mayfield aren't the way they should be. Just this
morning I saw a sign on the library I'd never seen before. I've
been in there a hundred times at least, and I'm sure that sign's

been there all one hundred of those times, but I never read it 'til today. You know what it said?"

The look on Maybelle's face told Lily she knew exactly what it said.

Still, Lily continued, "'Whites Only!' I couldn't believe it. Keeping books from folks seems downright cruel. I just don't understand. Now that I think about it, I never noticed a colored person in the library. But before today, I probably wasn't looking."

Maybelle gave Lily a pointed look.

"Mmmhmm, Miss Lily, things ain't fair. And the library feels like one of the most unfair things. I heard that some libraries in big cities are open to us folk, but not yet here in Mayfield."

"I'm just so... sorry, Maybelle," Lily replied, slowing the whisk. "I wish I could change it for you. And for Hazel."

"You seeing the unfairness and knowing you want things to be better is a good start, Miss Lily. But you oughta know, too, that white folk created this mess and white folk can help get us outta this mess, but only when they willing to let their hearts be changed. And the laws, 'course. White folk took away our polit-ical power, but they can't take away our voices. You know how women got the vote in the '20s?"

Lily nodded. She'd learned about the suffrage movement in school just this year.

"Them ladies had to raise hell, but it was the men who had to change the rules. So, we can gather and sign petitions and try to vote loudly enough to change the minds of the ones in power, but colored and white folks gonna have to work together on this. Both Hazel and you got the smarts to change this world someday, and I hope you will." And with that, Maybelle turned to the biscuits.

Lily thought about this. She was right. Of course, she was

right. But hearing Maybelle lay it out so plainly—that separation was the white folks' creation—made Lily feel all mixed up inside. What was her role in all of it? And then, what was her responsibility?

She left Maybelle when there were no more lumps in the pudding. Upstairs, she found her bedroom empty and plopped down on her bed. Just as she opened her book, she heard a little cough and a sad voice say, "'Scuse me, Miss Lily."

Lily looked up to see Hazel, cleaning supplies in hand, and right then she made an important choice. She would be brave. Brave for herself, brave for Hazel, brave for Maybelle.

"Hazel, come in. And please call me just Lily. I mean it."

Hazel looked unsure, but walked in and began dusting.

"Wait, Hazel, I got something for you," Lily blurted out. Hazel froze and slowly turned to look at Lily, who held out the library's copy of *Anne of Green Gables*. "I know you loved *The Hundred Dresses*, so I thought you might like this one. I've borrowed another copy from a friend and just started it. This one's from the library. Just make sure you get it back to me by the due date so Miss Nora doesn't skin my hide, okay?"

Hazel bit her lip. "Oh, I couldn't. I'm not even allowed to step foot in that library," she replied softly, her eyes downcast.

"I know." Lily walked toward her and held the book an arm's length from Hazel. "But you can borrow this one."

"Thank you, Miss... er... Lily," Hazel exhaled, taking the book tentatively. Lily gave her an encouraging smile.

"Don't worry, no one'll know but me. You can trust me." The two stood there for a minute before Lily grabbed a dust rag from Hazel's pail and said with a grin, "And, with both of us cleaning, it'll go twice as fast."

12

HAZEL

The next morning, Ma Maybelle went down to Wagner's Market to get a few things for the Wagners' supper, leaving Hazel alone in the house. Marianne and June were never there, and Lily was out with the dirty, squirmy boy from next door. Lily told Hazel she had to keep it a secret since his pa wasn't too keen on them being together. She'd also told Hazel they'd had a fight but not what it was about, and that she was giving him one more chance, for old time's sake.

"At least tell me where you're going?" Hazel had asked, a little nervous about being in the big house by herself.

"Just down to the creek," she'd said. "The boys are damming it up to make us a swimming hole!"

Expecting Lily to be out for a while, Hazel went up to Lily's room. She found the journal in the exact spot she'd left it, but peeked inside and saw that Lily had written in it the night before.

Dear Hazel,

Anne of Green Gables is so wonderful. I want to soak it all in, jump into the story, ride in the wagon right next to Anne (with an E), and just listen to her talk. That girl can talk! The description of the landscape and Green Gables paints such a beautiful picture in my mind. It must be the prettiest place in all the world. I feel bad that Anne hates her red hair. I hope she'll come around on that. Mine is just as red and just as curly and hard to manage, but I love it most days. It's different than my sisters' hair and when I look in the mirror, I'm reminded that I'm different than they are in more ways than one. For that, I am grateful.

I'm glad we are reading the book together. Just like Anne says, I feel like you and I are kindred spirits.

Yours sincerely,

Lily

HAZEL SMILED and was just about to open *Anne of Green Gables* for herself when she heard the front door slam open. She jumped up and ran downstairs.

The boy from next door held Lily in his arms; she was white as a sheet and clutching a very bloody pointer finger. He set her down gently and said, "I cain't stay here, Pa'll kill me. You understand?"

Lily nodded weakly and then swayed on her feet. Hazel ran to her side and held her up. The boy turned to Hazel and said, "You. Girl. Call Mr. Wagner at the store. Then Doc. A rattler bit her." He was out the door before Hazel could utter even a word.

Lily moaned and went limp in Hazel's arms. She carried Lily—who had started to shake—to the sofa and took a good look at her finger, the tip of which was punctured in exactly one place.

Willie, Jr. got bit by a rattlesnake just last year, so Papa had shown all of them what to do in the situation until a doctor could get there. But Papa had been with Willie, Jr. when he got bit, and Hazel had no idea how long ago the snake bit Lily. She secretly cursed that stupid boy. What a coward, more worried about his own rear end than Lily's life.

Still, Hazel knew what to do. She grabbed her cleaning pail, put Lily's finger up her to lips, and sucked as hard as she could. Warm, coppery liquid filled her mouth and she spit it all in the pail, trying not to think about Lily's actual blood being in her mouth. On the third spit, Lily's moaning got louder and she'd started sweating. And then, like she'd been summoned, Ma Maybelle walked in the front door. At the sight of Hazel and Lily, she dropped her grocery sack. A yellow onion rolled all the way over to Hazel's foot.

"Rattler," Hazel said. "I think I got all that I can, but she needs a doctor. I don't know how long it's been."

Hazel tied as tight a tourniquet on Lily's finger as she could with a rag she tore from her own dress as Ma Maybelle hurried to the kitchen and returned with cold water and towels. She told Hazel, "Go on to Doc Macintosh. It's just a few blocks. Run!"

With one last look at Lily, Hazel left the house at a full sprint. She knew where the white doctor's practice was but had never been inside. He'd made it very clear that he didn't serve Hazel's "kind." Whatever fear she'd have of bursting into a white doctor's clinic in normal circumstances was absent; she needed him to come for Lily.

Hazel's lungs burned as she ran, and she was surprised at the concern she felt for Lily. She hadn't even known her for very long. But they were connected all the same, by Wanda, by Anne, by the stories that occupied their thoughts. Hazel felt a sense of responsibility for Lily, as a human being, but also, she realized, as a friend. The worry she felt now that Lily might not be okay pushed her to run even harder.

The minute she flung open the door, it was like Hazel's good sense returned. White patients stood and stared at her. The lady at the desk dropped the phone that she'd had cradled to her ear, and started yelling for Doctor Macintosh. Later, Hazel realized how ridiculous this was. She was a twelve-year-old girl. What harm could she have done? But then, she was a *colored* twelve-year-old with a wild look in her eye, out of breath, and plus she probably still had some of Lily's blood around her mouth.

After what felt like ages, a man in a white coat came sauntering into the front room and yelled at Hazel. "What is the meaning of this?"

Still out of breath, Hazel stammered, "Rattlesnake bite... please... come quick... only a kid... feverish and..."

"Hold it right there, girl. You know I don't treat your kind. Go find Doc Harding. I got real patients waiting on me. Now get out." He wagged a fat finger at the door.

But Hazel stood her ground, her blood boiling. Was this really the time to worry about what color skin someone had? Just as Doc Macintosh turned his back, she spat out, "It's Lily Wagner, you know, the grocer's daughter? They live just two blocks away. Please come." Hazel was angry, but she was more worried about Lily than anything.

"Why didn't you say so?" he growled, before disappearing into the back. He returned a few seconds later with a black bag and gruffly told Hazel to lead the way. They walked quickly back to the Wagner house, Hazel a couple steps behind him, sputtering out all the things she'd already done for Lily.

When they got there, Mr. Wagner was running through the door, relieved to see Hazel with the doctor. Hazel stood in the corner of the room next to Ma Maybelle, who wrapped an arm around her shoulder. They watched as Doc Macintosh sliced Lily's finger at the bite and gave her a shot. Hazel buried her face in Ma's dress when Lily screamed. She didn't realize until now that tears were streaming down her face.

"We got her the antivenin in time, Clarke, but just barely. She should be fine after a few days, just swollen and sore. Keep the wound site clean and wrapped in a bandage."

Mr. Wagner nodded and reached out to shake the doctor's hand. "Thank you, Doc."

"Well, it wasn't all me. If that colored girl... " he nodded in Hazel's direction but would not look at her, "hadn't sucked some of the venom out and got me when she did, your girl would be a lot sicker than she is. Have a good day now, Clarke. I need to get back to the clinic."

When Mr. Wagner shut the door behind him, he turned to look at Hazel. "Hazel, right? I don't even know how to thank you." He wiped a hand across his cheek, taking some sweat and tears with it. He was so scared, Hazel realized.

"It's nothing, Mr. Wagner."

"It's not nothing to me."

Ma Maybelle smiled down at Hazel, her eyes filled with tears of pride, and the two watched as Mr. Wagner carried Lily up the stairs.

"You sure somethin' else, Hazel Clementine. Yes, ma'am, somethin' else," Ma said, giving Hazel a squeeze.

HAZEL WAS the hero in the Jackson home that night. As soon as she and Ma got home, Ma told everyone how smart and brave Hazel had been, how Lily could thank Hazel for her very life, how she'd spoken to the white doctor without fear and got him to do what she said. Willie Jr. knew how a rattlesnake bite felt, and was none too pleased to revisit that memory, but Glory and Hallie wanted Hazel to reenact every second. Hazel, finally free of the adrenaline that had flooded her veins before, laughed good-naturedly and played along with them. Mama gave Hazel a square of chocolate after dinner, which she shared with Glory when no one else was looking.

13

LILY

Daddy put an ice-cold washcloth on Lily's forehead and said, "Shh... you rest now, Lily Jo." His strong voice and the coolness of the cloth soothed her as she closed her eyes and drifted off.

After a fitful sleep, she woke again, guessing by the light that it was morning. Her whole right arm was puffed up like a giant marshmallow. Her pointer finger was bandaged on the end, and the pulse in it was too strong, unnatural. She tried to sit up, but her head felt funny, so she laid back on her pillow instead and stared at the ceiling.

She remembered Beau bringing her home but then leaving as soon as he got her there. *So much for "we'll still be friends,"* she thought with a frown. She remembered Hazel taking care of her and then a doctor. Just as she was considering how her summer was basically ruined, she heard a quiet knock on the door before it was pushed open.

"Hazel," Lily breathed. "Oh, I'm so glad to see you."

"I'm glad you're okay, Lily. Here, eat some breakfast. Ma Maybelle cooked the broth all night just for you."

Lily sat up slowly using only her good arm, and Hazel set a tray in front of her, with a steaming mug of broth and dry toast.

"You... you saved my life," Lily said, looking right into Hazel's golden eyes.

Hazel shrugged. "Just doing what I know how to do, I guess."

"Well, thank you all the same. I don't wanna think about what would've happened if you weren't here."

Hazel didn't respond, and once she saw that Lily could manage with her breakfast, she turned to leave. But Lily said, "Please, stay."

Hazel nodded and plopped down on the floor, thumbing through Lily's copy of *Anne of Green Gables*. "Do you want me to read to you?" she asked.

"Oh, yes, please!"

Even though Hazel had read farther than Lily, she turned to Lily's bookmark and began, "*Anne had been a fortnight at Green Gables before Mrs. Lynde arrived to inspect her.*" Hazel's voice was strong and confident, and Lily found herself completely swept up in the story.

When Lily had finished eating, Hazel moved to take the tray from her, but Lily said, "Please, don't stop reading."

So she didn't.

———

THE GIRLS SPENT their next two days doing just that: Lily in bed, nursing her arm, and Hazel reading aloud to her.

"Don't you just love Anne with an 'E'?" Lily asked her one afternoon.

"Oh, yes," Hazel replied. "She's so spunky and imaginative. And she feels her feelings right out loud. All the thoughts in her head come out of her mouth so easily!"

"I agree!"

"I like Diana, too," Hazel continued. "It's so nice that they have each other. Lily... do you have a bosom friend?"

"I thought I had Beau, but you saw him. He's nothing but a yellow-bellied coward."

Hazel nodded. "But what about anybody at your school?"

Lilly shrugged. "For most of my life it's just been me and Beau. I like being outside and playing games and sports and—now—reading, and lots of the girls at school act more like Marianne, prim and proper and scared to get dirty. What about you?"

"I don't have anyone to talk to about books or about what they want to do when they're grown, because nobody's interested in all that. They just tolerate school, but I love it."

"Well, we have each other then, Hazel. And I'm glad for it."

"Me too, Lily."

They sat quietly for a few minutes before Hazel said, "How do you think a little orphan girl with such a hard beginning at life can see the world with such wonder?"

"It's like she always chooses to see the good, even when she's in... what does she call it? The 'depths of despair'?"

"You're right. She does do that. I wish more people would be like Anne in that. It seems like sometimes hard things get folks down so much that all they can imagine are more hard things."

Lily nodded. She had a feeling Hazel's hard things looked a lot different than her own, but she didn't say anything more.

THAT NIGHT, Lily's arm was still sore but much of the swelling had gone down. She headed back to her favorite spot on the porch. The daylight slowly faded into dusk, leaving just enough light to read. She had only read about five pages when she heard Mother and Daddy talking in the sitting room through the screened window. Lily didn't mean to eavesdrop, but she heard Mrs. Shaw's name and her ears perked up. Stopping the swing, she sat very still to listen.

"... I just don't understand why Mrs. Shaw thinks this is appropriate. I mean, a colored girl, for heaven's sake, can you imagine? At the boarding house? What will people say? The woman already has a bit of a seedy reputation and now this?" Mother's shrill and shaky voice told Lily that she was worked up and maybe even frightened.

"Calm down, Miriam," Daddy interrupted. "First of all, it's only a rumor and second, there's no law against having a colored girl as a temporary boarder in town as long as the owner of the establishment allows it and the situation does not become permanent. Besides, Mrs. Shaw is a no-nonsense woman. She is quite firm about the girls' behavior and if this rumor is true, I'm sure she will be very choosy about the type of girl she takes in."

"And how do you know it's not against the law, Clarke?" Mother spat back at him, obviously surprised that her husband had gotten involved. Usually he preferred to stay out of the town gossip.

Daddy paused, and Lily imagined him shrugging his shoulders. "Mr. Roberts was discussing it in the store today. He's of the mind that it's certainly unprecedented, but not illegal, although he did say that Mrs. Shaw ought to retain a lawyer, just in case."

"And why should she do that if she's not doing anything wrong, Clarke? A lawyer would simply make her look guilty! And even out of the courts, she's going to look guilty all the same. I can't believe she's even considering it!"

"I'm not sure, Miriam, but I guess people can never be sure about these things. Angry mobs of people tend to be quite persuasive. A lawyer might be able to offer Mrs. Shaw some protection." Daddy's speech was unwavering. His was always the voice of reason in their home, and it tended to have a calming effect on others as well.

Mother said, quieter this time, "And why does this not bother you in the least? This is Mayfield, you know, not New York City or Chicago! We are Southerners, and Southerners have ways of doing things."

"A point well-taken, my dear. But why should things be deemed right simply because they are how they've always been? How can we move forward if we're stuck in our own traditions? And do our traditions benefit the people of our community or hinder them? This girl'll want to be a teacher or a nurse, Miriam. She won't be a common criminal, and she won't do anything to wreck the perfect picture that Mayfield claims to be."

Lily's jaw dropped. She hadn't ever heard her father speak to her mother like that. Not exactly angry, but firm, as if his mind was made up and there'd be no swaying him. Mother seemed to sense it as well, because she conceded in a much softer voice, "Oh, I suppose you're right, Clarke, she'll probably be perfectly nice and quiet. I just hope the women of Mayfield don't turn Mrs. Shaw into a pariah or make it a tense political situation."

"We shall see, my dear, we shall see," Daddy replied, and they settled into their chairs so he could read the newspaper and Mother could continue her needlepoint.

Lily exhaled. It felt like she'd held her breath the entire time. She couldn't believe what she'd heard. Mrs. Shaw taking in a colored boarding girl? Daddy standing up for her? Mother only concerned about how the town would react? As a family, they'd never discussed segregation, but Lily was happy to know her father's feelings on the issue. Still, Lily worried about Mrs.

Shaw, her new friend. Taking in a colored girl would be risky. It would challenge the Mayfield way of things. But she was also proud of Mrs. Shaw, the terribly misunderstood but kind-hearted woman. Lily hoped there'd be another delivery order to Mrs. Shaw's soon so she could check on her.

"Ahem," Lily heard a gruff voice clear his throat and looked up to see Mr. Adams on his porch, smoking a cigarette and staring right at her. Lily didn't know how she knew, but she could tell he had heard every word her parents said.

14

HAZEL

It was all anyone could talk about: the colored girl moving into Mrs. Shaw's boarding house. Lily had told Hazel the rumor, but the news made it all the way to Hazel's neighborhood on its own. She heard people at church whispering, and Mama and Papa talked about it when they thought everyone had gone to bed.

"You ask me, that white lady's putting that girl in danger over there," Papa's voice sounded small and unsure, which rattled Hazel.

"She might be putting us all in danger, depending on how folks react. But, it's kinda exciting right? Change is gonna happen one way or another, it can't stay like this forever," Mama's voice was steady and hopeful.

"Sure, but I hope that lady don't get nobody killed in the meantime."

"Oh, quitcho' worryin'," Ma Maybelle added from her place on the sofa where she'd been writing out her evening prayers. "We just gon' have to wait and see, that's all. No use worryin' 'bout things you can't control. Leave it up to the good Lord, now."

And that was that.

It did excite Hazel to think that someone was making a real change, doing something out of the ordinary, ruffling some feathers. But while it was exciting, it also frightened Hazel. She'd heard of riots and violence happening in other parts of the country where colored folks tried to enter places or even ride in the front of the bus where they weren't welcome. Hazel hoped the girl wouldn't be in danger.

A FEW DAYS LATER, it was confirmed. Mrs. Shaw, indeed, was taking in a colored girl, and the girl was moving in that very morning. Hazel and Ma Maybelle decided to leave early and take a different route to the Wagner home, one that would take them right past the boarding house. It was Ma's idea. Hazel had baked some fresh biscuits for the girl, hoping to give her a small comfort of home.

As they neared the boarding house, Hazel saw a small crowd gathered in front of the two-story colonial. A patrol car, she noticed, was parked across the street, with an officer looking out the window. Hazel's heart dropped and her palms began to sweat. The only time she saw police on her side of town was when someone was in trouble. She grabbed hold of Ma Maybelle's hand and looked up at her as if to ask, *are you sure you want to do this today?* But Ma pursed her lips, looked straight ahead, and kept walking.

A colored man and woman were unloading a car at the boarding house and a white woman, who had to be Mrs. Shaw, stood on the wide front porch. The white woman impressed Hazel. She seemed to simultaneously scowl at the crowd while kindly encouraging the family to bring the girl's things inside. Some of the onlookers looked angry. Others were just curious. They whispered in hushed voices, eyes wide, not wanting to miss anything. Ma Maybelle paused for a split second, as if rethinking her decision to welcome the girl, but Hazel felt another rush of determination flow through her and she marched up to the house. A young colored woman with beautiful wavy hair and a flawless ebony complexion came out the front door.

Hazel was close enough to hear the girl say, "Thank you, Mama and Papa. I think that's all. I know I'm gonna be just fine here." She flashed a confident smile at them.

Mrs. Shaw wrapped one arm around the girl. "Don't you worry, Mr. and Mrs. Grant, I'm gonna take good care of Hetty. She's safe with me. Y'all come in for a spot of breakfast before you head home."

Ma took this as their cue. She walked up the steps and held out the plate of still-warm biscuits, Hazel on her heels. If the folks on the porch were alarmed by a determined-looking colored woman traipsing up toward them, not one of them showed it. "Hetty is it? Welcome to Mayfield, child. I am Maybelle and this my granddaughter Hazel. We work for the Wagners, not too far down the road. Just wanted to say we glad you're here. Hazel made these fresh for y'all this morning."

Hetty smiled and gracefully took the biscuits. "Thank you both ever so kindly. They smell delicious."

Mrs. Shaw said, "They will go with our meal perfectly. Lily's always talking about your food. You tell her that I'll be wanting to see her soon."

Ma Maybelle nodded meaningfully. "We best be on our way and let you get settled in."

The folks on the lawn had been watching the whole

exchange take place and the patrol car hadn't budged an inch, but they parted to allow Ma Maybelle and Hazel to pass.

LATER THAT MORNING, Hazel was sweeping the front porch when she noticed an older man on the porch next door watching her every move. Despite his proper, clean-shaven appearance, Hazel could tell he was an unpleasant sort of fellow; his mouth was stuck in a perpetual grimace and his narrow eyes forced a scowl onto his brow. He made Hazel uncomfortable, like he was waiting for her to do something wrong. Hazel looked away, quickly brushed the last of the dust off the porch, and went inside.

Lily came in from doing a delivery right behind her, and she and Hazel once again plopped down on the floor in her room. Hazel read aloud the last two chapters of *Anne*. When she got to a certain part that made her choke on her words, she sneaked a glance at Lily, who had gone to the window. Lily didn't say anything, but Hazel saw her lift a hand to her face and wipe away a tear.

"'*God's in his heaven, all's right with the world,*' Anne whispered softly." Hazel closed the book.

"That's it?" Lily asked, incredulous.

"Yup."

"Oh, I don't want it to end! You know those books that you want to find out what happens but you still don't want it to end?"

"Yes, this one's exactly like that."

"Mrs. Shaw says there are more books about Anne. I'll check out the next one for us soon!"

Hazel grinned.

A loud clap of thunder interrupted their conversation and

soon after, they heard the sheets of rain coming down on the roof.

"C'mon Hazel, I have the perfect rainy-day thing for us to do!" Lily grabbed her hand and a few paper dolls and pulled her downstairs. She threw a white sheet over the dining room table and handed Hazel a flashlight. They both crawled underneath. Hazel felt cozy and like she was at home. She also felt like a child without a worry in the world, something she hadn't felt in a long time.

"Me and Beau used to do this all the time, act out the best stories like *Peter Pan*. See when you shine the flashlight at the paper doll, it makes a shadow on the sheet!"

Hazel giggled. What fun! Lily and Hazel acted out the best scenes from *Anne*: the Mrs. Lynde incident, the slate she smashed over Gilbert's head, the time she almost drowned, the time the girls jumped on Aunt Josephine. They laughed and laughed and laughed some more. Lying on their backs with their feet poking out from under the sheet, Hazel felt completely at ease.

When the laughter calmed and she could breathe again, Lily rolled over to face Hazel and propped herself up on one elbow. "You know what, Hazel? At first, I thought it would be hard for Anne to live with Matthew and Marilla, who didn't really need her. But it seems like—what does Marilla call it? Providence?—that she landed in exactly the perfect place for her. And it turns out, they needed her very much."

"I think so, too. It feels like everyone just couldn't help but love Anne once they got to know her."

"Yep," Lily agreed, and then held up her fingers, counting off each one, "Marilla, Mrs. Lynde, Diana's mother, even crotchety old Aunt Josephine."

"But not Matthew, no he loved her from the start. Gilbert, too," Hazel said.

"Oh yes! I imagine Gilbert to be ever so handsome."

"You know," Hazel said, not sure if she should continue, "you remind me a little of Anne."

"I do?" Lily said, raising an eyebrow. "How come?"

Hazel thought about the best way to tell Lily that she never stopped talking either and that she did a lot of acting before thinking, but in the end, she settled on, "Oh, just your red hair. And your imagination, too."

"That's funny, because I was thinking *you* reminded me of Anne."

Now Hazel was surprised. "Me? I pictured myself as more of a Diana."

"Oh, no, Hazel. You might be quieter than Anne, but you're no Diana. Remember when Anne saved Diana's sister when she had the croup? How she knew exactly what to do without anyone telling her? You did the same thing for me. You've got just as much Anne in you as I do."

The thought made Hazel smile, and she supposed Lily was right. Then she thought of something else.

"Lily? Did Anne make you think about Hetty, the new girl over at the boarding house? Do you think they'll make her feel welcome there? Make her feel like she belongs?"

Lily nodded thoughtfully. "Knowing Mrs. Shaw, yes. I just hope the rest of Mayfield leaves her alone. I also thought about Wanda. I hope the girls over there treat her better than Maddie and Peggy treated Wanda."

"Me, too. I hope Hetty has the same kind of grit as Anne," Hazel said, her voice low. "She's gonna need it. Hetty doesn't know it yet, but just by living there, she is giving a lot of folks hope that things could change someday. She's giving me that hope."

"Me, too," Lily said, squeezing Hazel's hand.

THAT NIGHT, Hazel lay in her bed, thumbing through *Anne of Green Gables* again, not quite ready to give it back to Lily. Glory walked in.

"Whatcha reading?" she wanted to know. "I loved *The Hundred Dresses* book. But oooh those girls were mean. Still, thanks for giving it to me."

"I'm glad you liked it," Hazel said, handing over *Anne* to her sister. "This one's good too. I'd let you read it, but I have to get it back to... um... its owner." She was glad when Glory didn't ask who the owner could be.

"What's it about?" Glory asked. Hazel told her the story, combing her fingers through Glory's braids, with an energy in her voice that she hadn't had before. Hazel talked and talked, trying to remember all the important details, until she heard Glory's breathing slow and felt her body relax against her own. Kissing Glory's forehead, Hazel left her to sleep and tiptoed out of the room to help Mama put the younger ones to bed.

Hallie asked Hazel to tell her a story next. As usual, Hazel made one up as she went, taking twists and turns that, quite honestly, made no sense. But Hallie squealed and begged for her to continue. Mama and Ma Maybelle stood in the doorway, listening to Hazel weave the complicated tale. Reading *Anne of Green Gables* had given her a new kind of confidence in her storytelling, and she let her imagination run like Anne's would have.

Hazel's story that night included more happiness, more friendship, and more kindness than usual, as if the layers of loneliness and fear were being peeled away from her characters. As if they were being peeled away from herself.

15

LILY

Lily had been pedaling around Mayfield making deliveries for Daddy. Just as she'd suspected at the beginning of summer, her sisters disappeared whenever deliveries needed to be made. June spent her days deep in the library stacks with her best friend Lucy or volunteering at Doc's clinic. And Marianne was always with her friends at a group swim in the creek or a picnic or a youth gathering at one of Mayfield's many churches.

For whatever reason, Marianne hadn't become an outcast with her friends like Lily had. Lily hadn't given it much thought, but when she did, she supposed Marianne spent a bit of time apologizing away her father's actions and batting her eyelashes at all the boys enough that they didn't worry about it anymore. The thought of her apologizing for Daddy made Lily hot with anger; he had done the right thing. Why couldn't Marianne see that?

"Well, good morning, Lily! How are you this fine day?" Rose said cheerfully when she saw Lily pull up to the boarding house.

"Doing just dandy, Miss Rose. How's everyone here?"

Lily knew that the new girl had moved in the day before. She didn't want to be nosy or intrude, but Lily was curious to meet her.

"We're all fine here. Mrs. Shaw's just making sure Hetty gets settled. I'm sure you've heard about our new boarder!" Lily searched Rose's face and tone for a hint of disapproval or worry at Hetty being colored, but she found none.

As if reading her mind, Rose added, "She's very nice, Lily." She lowered her voice and added, "Most of us are real glad she's here, but a couple of girls left as soon as they heard. Some of their parents didn't want them here anymore. And some left on their own. Mayfield's cranky old timers might not approve, but I assure you, it's all good here."

Lily had liked Rose when she first met her, but her affection grew even more. She sensed in Rose's statement a bit of mischievous defiance, as if making the town uncomfortable was fun. Rose beckoned Lily inside and asked, "Would you like to meet her?"

Lily nodded. She could feel the energy buzzing in the house. Usually, when she came for a delivery, the girls were out around town, or in their rooms studying. But that day it seemed like everyone was there, talking, laughing, and nibbling on the remains of breakfast. Lily was thankful Hetty was at least safe from hateful judgment inside the place that would be her home for a while.

As Rose and Lily emptied the last bag, Mrs. Shaw pushed open the swinging kitchen door followed by one of the most beautiful young women Lily had ever seen. Her smooth, dark skin was a shade darker than Hazel's, a deep ebony, and her shiny hair fell in gentle waves that perfectly framed her face. Even in the stifling heat and humidity, not one piece stuck out of place. But what struck Lily the most about her was her smile: bright white, confident, welcoming. She flashed it right at Lily.

"Well, hey there Lily!" Mrs. Shaw said. "I want to introduce you to Hetty, our newest boarder." Hetty held out her hand expectantly and Lily shook it.

"I'm honored to meet you, Lily. I've heard a lot about the redheaded delivery girl who stays around to talk books!"

Rose caught Lily's eye; Hetty was another reader. Lily liked her immediately.

"It's so nice to meet you, too. I hope you're settling in well."

"No complaints. Everyone's been very nice," Hetty said, her eyes shining. "I can't wait to meet my mentor teacher tomorrow. I'll do some summer work with her and then she'll show me how to start a brand-new school year. Her name's Miss Grace Hershey. Doesn't that sound like just the perfect teacher name?" Lily started to respond, but Hetty kept talking, reminding her a little of Anne. "Like she was just made for a classroom? Anyways, I'm so glad to know you like to read."

Lily grinned. Turning to Mrs. Shaw, she said, "I brought back *Anne of Green Gables* today!"

"Wonderful! Rose, be a dear and pour the four of us some iced tea and meet us in the library."

"Yes ma'am," Rose agreed, and Lily followed Hetty and Mrs. Shaw down the hall.

Lily felt like a grown up. Iced tea, two teachers-to-be, older and more sophisticated than she, and Mrs. Shaw, who was still a bit of a mystery to Lily. The four of them settled into plush armchairs.

"I feel just like Anne did when she visited Aunt Josephine in the city and they got to sit in the parlor. So fancy," Lily blurted out.

Mrs. Shaw laughed and said, "Oh, but to have a house as grand as Aunt Josephine's. You know Lily, sometimes I feel like

Aunt Josephine, although I'm quite a lot younger. I know I can be a grump sometimes, but I love what her character teaches us."

Lily couldn't help herself and let out a soft giggle. Mrs. Shaw raised a questioning eyebrow and Lily said, "I was just thinking about the first day we met. It was only a couple weeks ago, but now it feels like ages. You frightened me!" Filling in the other girls, she explained, "I interrupted her phone call because the stove had caught fire. She was so cross with me."

Rose and Hetty laughed good-naturedly, and Mrs. Shaw said, "Well, girls, perhaps I need to work on my first impressions. It seems I can be somewhat prickly."

"Well," Hetty chimed in. "You've been nothing but warm and welcoming to me."

Mrs. Shaw squeezed her arm and looked right into her eyes. "I'm glad because I want you to know that you are welcome here. You belong here. No matter what."

Lily took a picture in her mind then, wanting to remember the exact moment, Mrs. Shaw's exact words, the wrinkles around her eyes that were only visible when she wore a true, genuine smile. She wanted to tell Hazel later, in all the detail she could.

Hetty smiled gratefully and asked Rose if she'd help her finish unpacking. The two hopped up and walked out the door, arm in arm.

Lily took a deep breath. She felt that Mrs. Shaw had proven herself trustworthy, and Lily desperately wanted to talk to her about Hazel. "Thank you so much for trusting me with your book. I... I... want to ask you something." Lily bit her lip.

"Oh?" Mrs. Shaw looked up, interested.

"Who's Jim Crow?"

Mrs. Shaw's smile faded, and she closed her eyes, taking a moment to gather her thoughts, Lily figured.

"Jim Crow is not so much of a *who* but a *what*. It's the collective name for the laws we have that keep us separated from colored folk."

"So," Lily continued, wringing her hands. "Are you breaking the law by having Hetty here?"

Mrs. Shaw gave a sad little laugh. "No, dear, but I checked with an attorney just in case. All is well. You should know, however, that even though it's not against the law, there are still folks in town who are unhappy."

All Lily could do was nod; by now she was well aware of the displeased folks. Then she thought of something else she wanted to tell Mrs. Shaw.

"Also, I must confess that while I read your copy of *Anne of Green Gables*, I also checked it out from the library. For a friend... a friend who isn't allowed in the library."

Mrs. Shaw gave Lily a knowing look. "I see. You know that's against the rules, right?"

Lily nodded and said, "Yes, and I suppose it'd make some folks mighty unhappy too. But here's the heart of it, Mrs. Shaw. I don't think I did the wrong thing." Talking faster and staring at her shoes so she wouldn't see Mrs. Shaw's face, she added, "I returned the book to the library, just as if I'd read it, and no one will know that Ha... my friend... was the one who read it. We read it together while my arm healed. She loved it, too. It seems a terrible injustice to keep anyone from books."

Before Lily dared to look up, she heard Mrs. Shaw laugh and Lily let out her breath, relieved. "Oh Lily, I knew I liked you. Such passion! A lot like our Anne. I'm assuming your friend is Hazel, your maid's granddaughter?"

Lily looked at her with wide eyes. She hadn't been prepared to disclose Hazel's identity. "How'd you know?"

"Well, the two of them stopped by yesterday morning. It was very kind of them. She seemed like a polite girl, and courageous too. She barely batted an eye at the white folks standing around here looking for a story to tell their neighbors. I'm glad you're friends. Everyone needs a bosom friend, especially one they can read with. But, so you don't get in trouble, next time give Hazel my copy of the book and you can use the library's. Then you can tell the truth if anyone asks, okay?"

Surprising them both, Lily flung herself at Mrs. Shaw and hugged her fiercely around the neck. "Oh, I knew you'd understand! And not be angry with me! Thank you!"

Mrs. Shaw patted Lily's back, a low laugh in her throat, and asked, "Now, what shall you girls read next?"

And just like that, Lily headed home on her bicycle, her heart full, *The Secret Garden* riding safely in her basket. It was another favorite of Mrs. Shaw's, one with a strong heroine much like Anne. She couldn't wait to give it to Hazel.

THAT NIGHT WAS Mayfield's Founder's Day parade, the biggest event of the summer. This year's parade promised to be the best one since 1929, before the stock market crashed and everything went haywire. Even with the war in the Pacific still on and so many of the young men still gone, Mayfield would celebrate.

Marianne's youth group at the Methodist Church made a float. Of course, she'd be riding at the helm, her blonde hair flowing, her slender figure shown off by a fancy silken ball gown. June skipped the parade every year, thinking it a "silly old tradition." Lily loved it, but she usually loved it with Beau right beside her hooting and hollering. *Not this year*, she thought, willing the lump in her throat to go away. *Who needs him anyway?*

Right before Maybelle and Hazel got ready to leave, Lily

caught them at the door and said, "Maybelle, can Hazel stay longer tonight? We can watch the parade!"

Hazel's eyes made a *what are you doing?* face at Lily, and Maybelle caught her breath. Colored folk didn't attend the parade. Lily, sensing her hesitation, linked her arm in Hazel's and said, "Please, Maybelle! We'll stay here—on the balcony— the parade comes right down the street!"

Maybelle bit her lip, clearly worried, but Lily was too excited to pay attention. "How'll she get home tonight?"

Lily hadn't really thought it through, but blurted, "She can just stay with me! We'll drag my mattress out to the upstairs porch! Oh, it'll be such fun! Maybelle, pleeeeeease?"

Daddy and Mother walked in, dressed for the parade, and Lily pitched her idea to them. She saw her parents exchange a glance, but Daddy said, "Well, now, I don't see why not. She'll be safe here, Maybelle, and you'll be back in the morning. That is, if you're okay with it."

Maybelle stiffened but looked over at Hazel. "I dunno... Hazel?"

So quietly that Lily barely heard her, she said, "I'd love to, Ma Maybelle."

"Oh!" Lily cried. "This is going to be such fun!"

Maybelle pulled Hazel to her and knelt down, enveloping her in a tight embrace. She whispered something to Hazel that Lily couldn't hear, and Hazel smiled at her, saying, "I promise, Ma." Maybelle rose and smoothed down the apron over her skirt. As she left the Wagner house alone, she glanced over her shoulder at Hazel until she couldn't any longer, like her eye contact alone could keep Hazel safe and sound.

16

HAZEL

*Y*ou *be on your best behavior, now. Hazel. I mean it—you gotta be twice as good as you usually are. This a white man's home. We work here, but being here for other reasons is unheard of in this town. You gotta be your very best.* Ma Maybelle's words bore into her mind. She didn't know whether Ma Maybelle had agreed just because Mr. Wagner had allowed it and she didn't want to say a thing against him or because she knew Hazel did want to stay. She didn't have much time to think about it, though; she was too excited.

Hazel had not spent one night away from her family in her whole life. Her heart raced as she watched Ma Maybelle walk down the street alone. She wasn't exactly nervous; she knew she'd be fine. It was more of a feeling that she was growing up, putting some distance between herself and her childhood.

"Come on!" Lily yanked Hazel up the stairs and into her room. She pulled *The Secret Garden* out of her bag and handed it to Hazel. "I have the library's copy, but this is Mrs. Shaw's. She wants you to read it."

Hazel froze. "Wait. You told her?" she asked, an edge of

fear creeping up on her. She felt her palms start to sweat. Lily really had no idea how much trouble she could put Hazel in. What if Mrs. Shaw were to tell someone, the wrong someone? It was so easy for Lily to make these quick decisions—and they were done out of a wanting to be kind, Hazel supposed. But would Lily ever learn to stop and think about the danger she might be putting others in?

Lily blinked, not understanding the sudden change in Hazel. "Is that okay? She loved to hear that you like to read. And it was her idea for you to read her book so I wouldn't get in trouble at the library."

Hazel took a deep breath and was slow to answer. Lily was quiet, waiting. "I... I... guess. I just don't wanna cause trouble."

"You won't. From now on, you'll read her books and I'll read the library's. No trouble, no one else will know. I promise."

"Okay... if you're sure," Hazel replied.

Lily flashed her a big, reassuring grin. "I'm sure!"

"So, how's that reading contest going?" Hazel asked casually. She didn't want to let on that she really wished she could enter the contest, too.

"Oh, it's going. Beulah May has six already! Miss Nora and I had a nice chat about *Anne* and two other books I read last week, so that puts me up to four. Wait... how many books have you read?" Lily asked.

"Oh, I think eight. I hope you don't mind, but when you're not here, I read some of your books from the library. I never take 'em home, though."

"Of course I don't mind! Eight? Wow!"

"They were fine but not as good as the ones we've read together. Anyways, I hope you win, Lily," she said. "That Beulah May sounds awful. Just like Anne's mean old Josie Pye!"

"You're right Hazel, exactly like her! Snooty and arrogant and outright unpleasant!"

The girls dissolved into a fit of laughter, the awkwardness from before completely gone.

Mr. AND Mrs. WAGNER left the house just before dark to get to their preferred parade spot in front of the courthouse. The parade did indeed pass right in front of Lily's house, but the Wagners had made plans to meet up with a family friend from their church. Founder's Day was a big to-do in Mayfield, and as strange as it might sound, the parade was always held at night—its way lit by streetlights and sparklers and fireworks.

"Be good now, girls, and stay on the porch, you hear?" Mr. Wagner said firmly, but with a smile. Hazel knew it was a risk for him, too, to host a colored girl in his home outside of working hours. And the town was already full of whispers about the grocer.

June stayed in her room with the door shut, probably with a big textbook. Lily had told her that June never bothered with the parade, but Hazel didn't know if it was a political statement on June's part or just the fact that she preferred the quiet. As soon as the Wagners left the house, Lily turned to Hazel with a gleam of mischief in her eye.

"Come on, Hazel, we're gonna go to *my* preferred parade watching spot."

"Wait," Hazel said, her shaking voice unable to contain her worry. "We told Ma Maybelle and your parents we'd stay put. You don't know how people would act if they saw—"

But Lily cut her off. "No one will see us. It's dark, everyone's at the parade. We'll take back roads and stay hidden the whole time. Besides, the parade loses some of its *oomph* by the time it passes here."

"I'm just not sure..." Hazel started.

"Trust me, no one even knows about my spot. Well, except Beau, but he's probably with the boys tonight, and he didn't even really like it anyhow. We'll be free as birds! I swear it!"

Hazel looked at her friend's eyes—all lit up and sparkly—and her wild red hair, frizzing with the heat and excitement. Hazel knew it was dangerous. But she was tired of having to be so safe and good all the time. Lily never had to worry about such things. It was tempting—to spend the night pretending like the world was fair and right, that she and Lily were simply friends instead of one colored friend and one white friend.

Lily, noticing Hazel's hesitation, whined, "Pleeeeeeeeease, Hazel?"

And even though Hazel knew it was risky, and that they'd be disobeying all the adults, she agreed. Something about Lily's enthusiasm was contagious. They left the house without a word to June.

"You know, Hazel," Lily was saying as they walked down back alleyways to get to God-knew-where, "the story goes that Richard Mayfield, the town's first landowner and mayor, stumbled onto the land that now holds all the Main Street businesses. Have you heard this one?"

Hazel shook her head.

"Well, he was a slave-catcher on his way between two large tobacco plantations, looking for work, when he got lost in the dark and ended up following a creek to this little area tucked away and hidden by tall trees. Rumor has it he fell asleep at creek's edge, exhausted, and when he woke up was so taken with the beauty of his surroundings that he denounced his slave-catching ways. After that, they say he just stayed here. Had a family, invited others, and Mayfield was born!"

It was, Hazel supposed, an interesting story even though her stomach had lurched at the word "slave-catcher" and Lily hadn't even taken a breath to notice.

"Oh wow," Hazel said flatly. And then, "Hey Lily? Where are we going?"

"Oh! Someplace special! It's a secret!"

Lily pulled her along by the hand, and Hazel had to jog to keep up. After a few minutes, they reached what looked like an old, abandoned fire station. Surely, Lily wouldn't stop here. The wooden structure was cracked in many places and didn't look sturdy enough to hold a bird's nest. The roof had fallen in and was covered in moss. There were no lights this far off the road, but Lily said, "C'mon!" and walked around behind the building.

Hazel watched her step and tiptoed over weeds and pieces of wood that looked like they had broken off the old firehouse. She found Lily up about five steps onto a rickety ladder that led to a platform. Fortunately, the platform appeared to be more stable and newer than the rest of the structure. She shook her head—*this was crazy*—but followed Lily up the ladder.

"What is this place?" she asked once she and Lily were both seated comfortably on the platform.

"This is where we used to come to watch for enemy planes in the night, before they moved the watch-out to the bell tower of the Episcopal church. Usually the grown-ups do it, but Daddy let me come once. The firehouse burned down—remember? oh, the irony!—a couple years ago and they had to build a new one, but I think they figured it was far enough out of the way and had a good enough view of the sky and Mayfield to use as a lookout."

Lily turned out to be right. They could see every float in the parade, hear the band, see the soldiers who had lived through the war and come home early. They walked behind a huge American flag held out in front like a banner, tight against the breeze. Hazel saw people waving at the soldiers. Some of the soldiers, like her own Papa, were missing limbs or walked with canes.

"My Papa has a uniform just like those," Hazel said quietly when there was a lull in the music. She wasn't sure what made her say it, but being here with Lily, chatting away, must have given her some courage.

"Oh, really? He fought?"

"Yes—and lost his arm."

"Well then," Lily said in her speak-before-she-thinks kind of way, "he should be out here marching with the other soldiers!" She sat up straighter, like she was looking for him.

"Look at them," Hazel said, an edge to her voice that hadn't been there before. How could Lily not have known this? "Do you see any colored soldiers anywhere in the parade?"

Lily's energy quieted. "Oh, my. You're right. I've never noticed that before." Then, more to herself than Hazel, she said, "*Why* have I never noticed that before?"

"Because you didn't need to," Hazel said, so softly she wasn't sure Lily had even heard. Any further conversation was drowned out by the marching band and the fireworks passing, and the girls could feel the booms and the drums inside their own chests.

They sat together, munching on boiled peanuts and salt water taffy, until the last float passed their line of sight.

"What's your daddy like, Hazel? You haven't said much about him."

Hazel was hesitant; she'd seen how Lily worshipped her own father. "Papa's... well, he's not around much. He works out of town on a farm. The war changed him. He used to play and read with us, and he still does, but he's different now, quieter. You've seen him before, you know."

"I have? When?"

"That cold voting day, a while back? He got beat up that day."

"That was your papa?" Lily said, eyes wide. "That girl... was you?"

Hazel just nodded, and Lily said, "I can't believe it."

"He tried again, you know, just last year. And even with his Army uniform on, missing the arm that he'd given to protect this country, they still didn't let him vote."

Lily breathed out something that sounded like "so sorry" but her words danced on the air, getting lost in the warm breeze, and she wouldn't look at Hazel for a long moment. They were both quiet then, sitting in the dark night watching parade helpers clean up firework debris and candy wrappers left behind.

Hazel was the first to speak again. "That was fun, Lily. Thanks for bringing me here." Her words snapped Lily right back into her usual self.

"You bet! I don't like being up close anyway, it's too noisy. Let's go home. Have you ever played Monopoly? I bet you'll beat me!"

THEY WERE ALMOST BACK to the Wagners' when Hazel heard a "Psssssst! Lily!" coming from the large holly hedge that separated her neighbor's house from the street.

Lily stopped. "Beau?"

The bush rustled and out popped the dirty boy who Hazel hadn't seen since the snake bite incident. He smiled at Lily, but his face changed to complete shock when he saw Hazel standing next to her.

"Beaumont Lee Adams, you go back inside! I don't ever want to see your face again!" Lily yelled at him.

"Wha... what?"

"I could've *died*, you dummy! You're such a coward. Lucky Hazel was there." Lily hooked her arm in Hazel's and pulled her close.

Beau set his mouth into a firm frown. Then he scrunched his nose and eyebrows and said, "Well then, have fun with that *colored* girl. I thought it was just your daddy, but I guess it's you, too!" Turning his back to the girls, he pushed his way back through the hedge.

Lily tossed a handful of rocks over the bush, hoping one would hit its target, and she screamed, "You don't know *anything* about *anything*, Beau!"

Hazel bit her cheek to keep from laughing, but she couldn't calm the fear that pulsed in her chest. *Beau could say something to his father. The Wagners would find out they left. Ma Maybelle could get in trouble.*

Lily was shaking and pulled Hazel up into her own house, right into an angry June.

"And just *what* do you think you two are doing?" she demanded, her hands on her hip, her face pink and splotchy. "I'm supposed to be watching you for Mother and Daddy, you know."

Lily's cheeks reddened. "Oh, come on, June, we are fine."

"Fine? Fine? Do you *know* what people of this town would think if they saw you two together? Do you *know* what they'd say about Daddy and his store? Even more than they already do? I know you're too young to remember the Klan, burning crosses in colored folks' front yards for much less than two little girls walking around together. But I do! You think a brick through a window's bad? Just ten years ago, right here in Mayfield, a colored man was strung up for just looking at a white lady sideways! Mother and Daddy tried to hide it from me, but I heard anyway. Things haven't changed that much!"

Drops of spittle flew from June's mouth as she spoke. Hazel was surprised, and listened with wide eyes. She'd never heard June speak this many words strung together in the whole time she'd worked for the Wagners. She also felt a kinship with June, the oldest sister, trying desperately to protect the younger ones.

"No one saw us," Lily lied. "It's fine." Hazel trained her eyes on the floor to avoid betraying Lily.

"You better *hope* you're telling the truth. You just wait 'til I tell..."

"Well you can't do that now, June," Lily said with a smirk. "You were supposed to be in charge of us, right? That would make you look like a terrible babysitter."

June opened her mouth to speak but shut it again. Hazel imagined she could see smoke coming out of June's ears, and she was a little afraid she might explode.

"Fine," June said through gritted teeth. "But you owe me."

Seeing Hazel's face, June softened a bit and turned toward her. "Just so you know, I don't have a problem with you two being friends. I just need my dumb *sister—*" she turned back to Lily, "to understand the danger you both were in."

"Okay, I get it," Lily said, her voice quieting. She turned to Hazel, looked her in the eye, and said, "I'm sorry I didn't think about it that way."

Hazel nodded, but she was glad, in a way, that June had gotten mad and explained the danger to Lily so she wouldn't have to later. Hopefully June had scared Lily enough to keep her from being careless again. And even though Hazel had been nervous, she had to admit to herself that she did have a good time.

"Now go upstairs and look like you've been here all along

before Mother and Daddy get home," June said, her anger still present but quieter.

Lily didn't say anything as she and Hazel worked together to pull her mattress onto the upstairs porch. She still didn't say anything until they had covered the mattress with a sheet and the fluffiest pillows they could find. Hazel was glad there was a large and healthy live oak standing between the Wagner house and Beau's—she didn't want any chance of him seeing them up there.

Inside, Lily found a nightgown for Hazel and said, "Hazel. I'm so sorry about Beau. His pa is the meanest man in Mayfield. And sadly, it looks like he won't be far behind." A quiet pause, and then, "Are you okay?"

"Yeah, but Lily, we were really lucky not to see anyone else. And that boy frightened me. What if he tells his pa?"

Lily paused, but then said confidently, "He won't. He's more scared of his pa than he is mad at me. Try not to worry, okay? Here, put this on, I'm gonna go get us some snacks," and she left Hazel alone.

Hazel did try not to worry, but while she knew it was an easy thing for Lily to say, it was a much harder thing for Hazel to do.

The girls ate more peanuts and some of Ma Maybelle's cookies. In the comfort of Lily's porch, Hazel felt her heart unclench a little at a time. They played Monopoly but got bored before they could determine a winner. They looked through Lily's collection of Big Little Books. Hazel's favorite was called *Flash Gordon*; it was full of adventure and action and pictures.

Mr. Wagner poked his head out once to see how the girls were doing and to say goodnight and then Lily read the first chapter of *The Secret Garden* aloud. When she stopped, she said, "Oooh, I'm so mad at that Beaumont I could spit. The last time I was this mad at him, I was in first grade and slapped his face when he flipped up my dress."

"You should get him back, Lily. He really was such a coward and he doesn't seem like a very nice boy."

"Yes!" she said. "And I know just the thing! You best stay here. I'll be right back!"

In true Lily fashion, she threw one leg over the edge of the porch and Hazel watched in horror as she shimmied down the lattice that held the ivy plants. It was too dark for Hazel to see what her friend was up to, but she heard the tinkling of glass for a few minutes and then she heard Lily's heaving breaths as she climbed back up the trellis.

"Wha... what'd you do?" Hazel asked.

"You'll see!" Lily said with a wild look in her eye. Hazel giggled.

Right as Hazel's eyes got heavy, and she was about to drift away to sleep, Lily said quietly, "Hazel, I really am sorry I didn't think more about how dangerous us going tonight was for you." Hazel didn't want to tell her it was okay, so she turned to face Lily and just said, "Thanks." Then both girls fell back on their pillows and fell asleep.

THE NEXT MORNING, the girls were awakened by a loud crash, the sound of broken glass, and a "Gosh darn it!" in the same voice that had yelled at Lily the night before.

"Yes! It worked!" she whispered.

"What'd you do?" Hazel asked again.

"I stacked up all their milk bottles and ours, right next to the door. Beau's pa always makes him go get the paper first thing!"

The girls stifled their giggles. And later, when Hazel went

to greet Ma Maybelle at the door, she glanced over and saw Beau sweeping up the glass, muttering to himself, a look of disgust on his face.

"You good, Hazel-girl?" Ma asked, looking her up and down, as if examining her for injury.

"I'm good, Ma. It was fun. But I'm glad to see your face. And, I'm mighty hungry."

Ma laughed and wrapped Hazel up into a tight hug.

Hazel noticed that Ma held on a little longer than usual when she hugged her that morning. Or maybe it was Hazel herself who lingered in Ma's strong arms. She'd had fun with Lily, but now that the sun was up once again and Ma was back and they'd go on about their regular business, Hazel felt like she could finally relax. She'd done what Ma had told her, been on her best behavior—besides leaving the house, of course, which was more Lily's doing anyway—and Hazel didn't realize until that moment how very exhausting it had been to stay mindful of every single action, every word that came out of her mouth. She let herself stay in Ma's arms for just a second longer before they got to work.

17

LILY

Thursday morning, Lily found Daddy in the kitchen, ready for breakfast. He grinned and sipped his coffee in silence as he waited for the others to come down. Once all the Wagners had stumbled in, he boomed cheerfully, "Pack your bags! We're going to the Inlet for a long weekend! I've got it all set up for Marty to run the store, and Aunt Margaret knows we're coming!"

The girls cheered. They all loved the Inlet. Mother gave Daddy an amused smile and planted a kiss on his cheek.

"What a wonderful surprise, darling."

Lily raced upstairs to get ready. She packed her swimsuit and shorts and then tossed some, but not all, of her library books into her bag, including *The Secret Garden*. Her gaze fell on Hazel's notebook, and she decided to give it back to Hazel for the weekend. They hadn't written to one another in some time, preferring to talk in person instead, but Lily thought Hazel might want to write about their newest book.

Maybelle and Hazel arrived at their usual time, and Lily found them in the kitchen preparing a basket of provisions for the trip. Daddy had surprised them, too. The trip meant that they had the rest of the week off.

On her way out, Lily slipped the notebook to Hazel, who hid it in her apron. "There are some books in my room. Take them home if you like!"

Hazel grinned and gave Lily a tight squeeze. "Have fun!"

———

THE HOUR-LONG DRIVE PASSED QUICKLY. June and Lily spent the time reading, and Marianne chattered the whole way about her friends; who was sweet on whom, who was the most popular or most stylish, who told the best stories. Lily suspected that no one was actually listening. Daddy drove and held Mother's hand when he was not shifting gears, and Lily felt at peace. She lost herself in her book, becoming acquainted with Mary Lennox and marveling at Misselthwaite, the dark and mysterious English manor that was full of secrets.

Before long, Daddy pulled up to a beautiful old house. Aunt Margaret's estate on the water was one of Lily's favorite places on earth. The Wagners hadn't visited for a full year, and it was evident that time had passed. The white paint had faded to a pale gray, and the front steps needed tending. A dark green moss crawled its way up the Victorian columns and chimney. The porch was missing a board, and they had to tiptoe around it. Even so, to Lily it felt like coming home.

Greta, Aunt Margaret's maid, greeted them at the front door and showed them to the back porch where Aunt Margaret was waiting with a tray of sweet iced tea and cookies.

"Y'all made it! Come set awhile!" She hugged each Wagner in turn, and looked the girls up and down.

"Oh, ladies, you are just as lovely as ever. Lily, you're getting so tall. Marianne, what a beauty you are! And June, how are your studies going? I know how much you love your books."

"Very well, thank you," June replied.

Daddy interrupted and asked what kinds of things he could do to help her around the house while they were there, and the girls used the opportunity to take their things to their rooms.

Lily climbed two flights of stairs to the highest bedroom, her very own at the Inlet, home to a single twin bed, a night-stand, and a lamp. It wasn't much to look at and it was the hottest room in the house, but it was all hers. A small round window faced the water and Lily cracked it open, hoping to entice a breeze.

Once they had put away their things, they joined Aunt Margaret for lunch on the porch. Unlike the house, Aunt Margaret hadn't changed a bit. She was a quiet woman, often deep in thought, and Lily thought her a bit lonely. Uncle Albert had died only five years before in a tragic automobile accident, leaving her all alone in the giant house.

AFTER LUNCH, everyone sipped sweet tea and grabbed a rocking chair, watching the sunlight glimmer on the water just past the old weeping willow. Lily thought that the weeping willow couldn't have been more aptly named. Ever since she'd read *Anne of Green Gables*, she paid more attention to the names of things for Anne often renamed things when she could think of better ones. But the weeping willow simply embodied sadness, its arms hanging low to the ground, swaying gently in the sea breeze as if part of a long, melancholy dance.

Lily rocked lazily as she listened to Aunt Margaret tell the news of the Inlet.

"You remember old Joe Spier, the best fisherman and

shrimper the Inlet has ever seen? He finally proposed to Miss Fanny, the owner of the diner! The wedding's going to be a right spectacle, everyone will come, of course."

"Well I do hope they find someone else to do the food," Marianne added. "It would be *so* tacky to cater your own wedding!"

Mother looked sternly at Marianne, who shrugged and said, "What? You know I'm speaking the truth."

"Even so," Daddy said, "not every truth need be spoken aloud, Marianne."

Aunt Margaret continued like there was no interruption at all. "And poor Sister, you know, my neighbor? She lost her husband to a stroke in May."

Lily had no trouble remembering Sister. She made the best pecan pie in all of South Carolina, and everyone in the Inlet knew it.

"I'm thinking of asking Sister to move in with me so we'd have each other. Except, of course," she lowered her voice, "we'd have to let Sister's help go. No sense in paying two of them when Greta can handle this old place just fine."

Lily thought of Greta, her bony fingers twisting with age, her back hunched from all the work she'd done over the years. How she'd have two old biddies to take care of that would double her workload. "Is that really..." she started, but Aunt Margaret kept on.

"Oh, and we have the nicest new minister in town! He and his wife, Rachel—such a sweet young thing—come for dinner regularly. I want to make sure Greta still feels needed and useful, you know," Aunt Margaret said. Between meals for Aunt Margaret and all that house to clean, Lily suspected that Greta had plenty to do, but she bit her tongue. Obviously, Aunt Margaret was enjoying carrying the conversation for all of them.

The Wagners, in turn, filled Aunt Margaret in on all the Mayfield news. She made a face and tsk-tsked when Marianne told her about Hetty at the boarding house. "Oh Lawd, I hope they don't rain trouble down on that town. Mayfield sure doesn't like to change! Isn't she worried about, you know, diseases and such? Lord knows colored folks aren't as clean. No one's sure what kind of illnesses those people carry with them. And what if she's, you know, *noisy* or puts her eyes on the Mayfield football boys?"

June choked on her tea, then, and Daddy had to thwack her on the back. To his sister, he mumbled, "I guess she's not that worried, Maggie," before changing the subject.

Lily, like June, was caught off-guard. How could dear Aunt Margaret think those things about colored people? Besides Greta, how many colored folks could Aunt Margaret have even been around in her lifetime? There weren't that many at the Inlet. And how could Daddy not speak up? He certainly didn't agree with what Aunt Margaret had said. But he wouldn't meet Lily's eye.

She opened her mouth and started to say, "I know Mrs. Sh..." but Marianne cut her off, asking to go out and search for her friends. Even at the Inlet, she was popular and social and couldn't be content to sit still with the rest of the family. Mother and Daddy went upstairs for a nap, and June, Lily, and Aunt Margaret settled into their usual reading spots. It was hotter than blazes, but the screened-in porch was situated just right to let in a light breeze.

The Secret Garden was set on a moor in England and could not be more different from her current spot on the porch. The moor was cold and dreary and mysterious, and Lily got completely lost in the story. When a bead of sweat dripped onto her page, Lily set the book down and wandered barefoot out onto the long wooden pier.

Aunt Margaret's house sat about fifty yards from the Inlet, and the pier reached into the water even now, at low tide. Lily breathed in the air, full of salt and swamp grass and fish. During low tide, you couldn't walk along the water because of the oysters and broken shells that lined the sand. Barnacles climbed their way up the pier and seaweed wrapped its spindly fingers around the wooden legs, so Lily stayed safely on the top of the pier, her legs dangling.

Although the scenery was beautiful, it was the calm and laid-back nature of life at the Inlet that drew Lily in. She thought of Mayfield, always busy, people always around. At the Inlet, folks moved slower. They liked to sit still and watch the tide go in and out from their porches. Lily laid back and closed her eyes, drank in the warm sun on her face, and listened to the gentle lapping of the water and the calls of red-winged black-birds among the cattail reeds.

After supper that night, they gathered on the porch with peaches and cold sweet cream to listen once again to Aunt Margaret tell the story of Alice the ghost. Lily loved a good ghost story, and Aunt Margaret told great ones, but something had changed. Lily found herself wondering if from now on she'd hear everything Aunt Margaret said differently, as if her misguided ideas about colored people would make Lily see her as a different person entirely. Aunt Margaret's voice broke into her thoughts.

"Alice Belin Flagg was the most beautiful girl to ever walk the roads of the Inlet. All the gentlemen noticed her, but none more than a certain young turpentine dealer. He was hand-some and rugged and doted on Alice. She adored him.

"Alice lived in this very house with her brother, Dr. Allard Flagg, and her mother, who was still in mourning over the loss of her dear husband. Both disapproved of the match, asserting that the young man was beneath Alice's station. But Alice was headstrong, accustomed to getting her own way. Of course, she fell in love with him, and he proposed to her with a small gold ring, right under that willow in the yard."

Aunt Margaret pointed a finger out into the yard, and everyone's eyes followed her gaze to the tree. The slightest breeze caused a few of the leaves to flutter, and Lily felt a chill go up her spine.

"Alice wore the ring on a chain around her neck to keep it hidden from her brother and mother. That winter, though, Alice was finishing her term at college in Charleston when she became ill with malaria. Dr. Flagg was sent to retrieve her, and he brought her back home, to this house. As he tended to her fever, he found the necklace and grew very angry. So angry in fact that he ripped the ring off the chain and flung it into the Inlet, right off the pier."

Everyone gasped politely, making Aunt Margaret smile.

"Alice died that very day, still wailing about the missing ring. People say she came back to haunt the Inlet. And that even after her brother died, she stayed. People say they've seen her, in a white dressing gown, searching the house and the water for her lost ring."

Aunt Margaret paused for effect and the girls leaned in closer.

"They say if you visit her grave, you can walk around it thirteen times backward and lie down and you'll be able to commune with her spirit. I even know a girl who, in the mere presence of Alice's grave, suddenly had her own engagement ring flung from her hand!"

"Oh Maggie," Daddy chuckled. "That story gets better and more ridiculous the more times you tell it!"

Aunt Margaret gave him a serious look and said, "Laugh all you want, dear brother. But just the other day, a man rapped on my door and said he saw a young girl running through the azaleas in an old-fashioned white dress, looking frightened. But once he got into the yard, she had disappeared."

"Oooooh!" the girls squealed in unison.

"I told him, 'Ah, don't you worry sir, that's just the Inlet ghost, Miss Alice Flagg.' As an out-of-towner, he'd never heard of Alice. He went white as a sheet and backed up real slow 'til I couldn't see him anymore."

The story was a legend around the Inlet, and people interested in the macabre came from all over to see "Alice's house" to try and catch a glimpse of her determined spirit still haunting the old mansion. When Lily was younger, the story had terrified her, and she could barely sleep in the attic, which had once been Alice's room. Now, however, she thought of it as a sad, yet romantic, fantasy of the family who had once lived there.

The Wagners broke into their usual Alice-the-ghost conversation. Daddy and Mother tried to explain the science—and religion—of why ghosts couldn't be real. June scoffed at the fact that any woman would lose her mind over a boy in such a way that she couldn't rest in eternal peace. Marianne was furious that Alice's brother couldn't recognize true love. And Lily, for her part, simply looked out at the water, searching for a glimpse of Alice.

She also wondered, perhaps for the first time, why Alice's brother had been so set against the engagement. So the young man didn't make as much money as a doctor, or have a certain title, but why did that mean he wouldn't make a suitable husband? Before there were "colored' and "white" sides of towns, were there "poor" and "wealthy" ones? This thought made her think of the servants in *The Secret Garden* and then Lily wondered if the strange crying Mary Lennox was hearing could be a ghost, so she pushed her questions to the back of her mind, said goodnight, and crept upstairs to read by lamplight.

18

HAZEL

"Whatcha gonna do with your afternoon off, Hazel girl?"
"Well, I got some books to read, so I'll probably find a quiet place and do that for a while," she replied.

Ma laughed, "You best stay outta the house, then, child, Lawd knows there's always a mess a' noise there."

"What about you?"

"Well now, I think I'll go on down to Ida's to play some cards and go visit some of the poor and ailing from the church. They always love Ma Maybelle's stories!"

Hazel smiled, "Oh yes! And Ma? I'm really glad you took me to work at the Wagners'. I like being there with you."

"Me too, child, me too."

They climbed onto the bus and took seats in the back. As they neared their neighborhood, Hazel spotted the elementary school from the window, which made her think of Miss Grace. She decided to stop in and see her teacher before she went home.

Not finding Miss Grace at home, she tried the school instead. The door to Hazel's old classroom was propped open to let a breeze in, and Hazel heard voices inside. She peered in and spotted Miss Grace with Hetty. They turned and noticed her at the door. "Hazel!" Miss Grace exclaimed. "Come in! I want you to meet somebody."

Hetty smiled. "Actually, I believe we've already met. It was you and your grandmother who brought those delectable biscuits to the boarding house, right?"

Hazel nodded shyly.

"Hazel was one of my best students," Miss Grace told Hetty proudly. "A strong reader and questioner of things. The best kind of pupil to have." To Hazel she said, "Hetty is working with me to learn all my tricks, and the school will try to find her a permanent place in the fall."

Hazel's shyness flew away. "Oh, I hope you'll get junior high, Miss Hetty! I'm glad you're learning from Miss Grace. She's the best teacher I ever had."

"Well, thank you Hazel, but teachers can't be good without good students," Miss Grace replied. "What brings you by today? I thought you'd be working at the Wagner house."

"Mr. Wagner took the family to the Inlet and gave us a couple days off. I just wanted to drop by to tell you I read another book, and I wondered if you knew it. *Anne of Green Gables?*"

Hetty raised an eyebrow.

"I do!" Miss Grace said. "I read it during teacher's college. What did you think?"

"I loved it. And so did Lil... my friend who also read it." Hazel didn't know how much she wanted to share about Lily. In the next moment, however, she realized she didn't have much choice.

"Are you talking about Lily Wagner? The charming little grocery delivery girl?" Hetty asked. "I met her at the boarding house the other day! She's very bright."

Hazel looked down at her feet. "Yes'm. Lily gave me the book to read from the library. I didn't want to tell because I don't want trouble for her."

"Your secret's safe with us," Miss Grace said. "But make sure you girls are careful. I'd hate for the wrong person to find out."

Hazel explained the solution Mrs. Shaw had come up with.

"Probably for the best," Miss Grace said. "Now, tell me what it's like being friends with a white girl. White and colored folk in this town don't usually mix well."

"Lily is a lot of fun," Hazel started out. "And she thinks about things I don't think many white folks my age think about. She thinks us not being allowed in places—especially the library—is unfair. But, just like me, she doesn't know what to do about it."

Miss Grace smiled and sat back in her chair. "Well, Hazel, I'd say you're off to a good start. It can never hurt, getting to know other folks and learn how they feel about things. That only helps us understand each other better."

WHEN HAZEL LEFT THE SCHOOLYARD, she didn't walk right home. Instead she found her old oak tree. Hoping the shade would bring some relief from the heat, she laid down on the grass underneath its long branches and wide leaves. She pulled *The Secret Garden* out of her bag and opened it. That hopeful, anything-can-happen feeling rose in her chest again. The feeling that what lies in the coming pages could change her life, make her cry, grow her faith in people. The feeling that this new story would take her someplace new, someplace she'd probably never visit, but someplace she'd be familiar with by the book's end just the same.

"*When Mary Lennox was sent to Misselthwaite Manor to live with her uncle, everybody said she was the most disagreeable-looking child ever seen.*" And just like that, Hazel was gone, the heat of the day fading into a swampy mist.

Dear Lily,

I'm glad Mrs. Shaw picked The Secret Garden *for us. It's so mysterious. When I first started, I thought Mary was just like Anne right away: Mary's an orphan, she moves to a new place with a new family, neither one is wanted at first. But when I got further, I saw that the two girls are very different. Anne is wanted by Matthew right off, where nobody seems to want Mary. I can't hardly blame them, though. As much as I liked Anne when I met her is as much as I dislike Mary Lennox. She is rude and spoiled and cranky. She has such a bad attitude, the exact opposite of Anne's sunny one. And Misselthwaite Manor, with the gray clouds and dark, dank hallways, is so different from the cheerful and warm Green Gables. I can't blame Mary too much though, because her parents never taught her proper behavior or that she was loved and belonged somewhere. And, the place she has come to feels so dreary and sad. I hope something good happens to her. All the mystery around the garden has me very interested. I can't wait to read more.*

What's the Inlet like? I've never seen the ocean but would love to someday. I hope you're having a wonderful time.

Until next time,
    Hazel

19

LILY

The rest of the weekend at the Inlet was indeed wonderful. They walked as a family to the ice cream shop on Main Street once a day and spent the mornings sitting on the shore, searching for shells on the beach, fishing off the pier, and building castles in the sand. During the hottest part of the day, Lily rocked in the porch swing and read for hours while the others napped.

One afternoon, Aunt Margaret, whose drawing skills matched her storytelling ability, sketched a charcoal picture of Lily, curls blowing around her face, a thick novel in her hand, freckles spotting her fair skin. Lily had been so focused on the book that she didn't notice until Aunt Margaret presented her with the completed drawing.

"To keep?" she asked. Aunt Margaret nodded, pleased by Lily's delight. But again, her heart sank a little. It occurred to Lily then that, while Aunt Margaret hadn't actually changed, Lily's understanding of her had. She wondered if finding out the truth about beloved adults, even truths that were hard to swallow, was simply a part of growing up. She wished with all her might that Aunt Margaret hadn't said what she did.

On Saturday, Lily went out in a small boat with Daddy to fish. She was happy to go with him; the other girls turned up their noses at the offer and Mother never went. After about an hour without a single nibble, they were ready to call it quits. The oppressive heat had Lily convinced that the fish were down in cooler water, much deeper than their lines could reach. She was surprised, then, when she felt a strong tug on her line. So strong that she almost toppled right out of the boat. Luckily, Daddy caught her and steadied her hand on the rod.

"Reel 'er in, Lily Jo!" Daddy shouted. Together they pulled and pulled, slowly reeling in the line. Finally, they saw something big and dark looming just below the surface of the water. After one final pull, they both cried, "Oh!" when they saw what was hanging on the end of the line.

A stingray!

Lily spied the sharp barb at the end of its tail and tried not to panic. She'd heard horror stories of people getting on the wrong side of a stingray and she was not eager to join their ranks. Rather than try to salvage the hook and risk certain injury, Daddy slashed the line with his knife. The ray hit the water with a splash and flipped its tail as it swam away. They erupted with laughter, relieved to have escaped disaster but glad to have a story to tell.

"Good thing Greta wasn't counting on any redfish for dinner, or we'd have sorely disappointed her!" Daddy said with one more laugh. "Are you having a good weekend, Lily Jo?"

"Yes, Daddy. This was such a fun surprise!"

"I'm glad. I want you to know that I appreciate all your hard work at the store. Make no mistake, I know your sisters aren't helping one single bit, unless Marianne comes in to bat her eyes at good ol' Marty," Daddy said, chuckling.

"It's actually been fun, getting out and meeting the neighbors. The deliveries have introduced me to some great people."

Daddy raised an eyebrow. "Like who?"

"Well my favorites so far have been Mrs. Shaw and the girls at the boarding house," she said brightly.

Daddy smiled. "Oh really? I thought you were scared of her after the little fire incident. You said you'd never go back."

"Well, it turns out, she's really a nice lady once you get to know her. And interesting, too." Lily told him about Mrs. Shaw's library, meeting Rose and Hetty, and all the reading she'd done.

"What'd you think about Hetty? She's the colored girl there, right?" Daddy asked, genuinely curious.

Lily paused before she spoke. "She's real nice. And brave too. Hazel told me that they stopped by the boarding house the morning she moved in, and Hetty didn't worry a bit over the neighbors who had gathered to stare at her."

Daddy grinned. "Brave is a good word for it. Mrs. Shaw too, I suppose. It's not easy to ruffle feathers in our town, you know."

"Yes, but Daddy, why is that? I keep hearing that Mayfield isn't ready for change, but plenty of change happens all the time. Mr. Blackburn opened a new pharmacy, and no one blinked. Jean's started opening for supper and no one cared. Why's it so bad for a colored woman to live in a white boarding house?"

Daddy furrowed his brow, like he was thinking hard about how to respond, but like he also felt a bit uncomfortable. "Well now Lily Jo, it's 'cause folks have been living separate for as long as anybody living can remember. They don't know any different. It's the law here in South Carolina, and most folks just follow the law to stay out of trouble."

"But Daddy, colored folks are just people like us. They

have darker skin, and they talk differently than us sometimes, but they're just people."

He softened as he looked at his youngest daughter. "You see, darlin', and this is hard to say aloud, but the best way I can explain it is that it goes back to slavery, when colored folk worked the land, and we fought that big war over it. Then later, when white folk decided to keep things separate, and Jim Crow laws came to be, people kept on believing that white folks were better, more important than colored folks. And when ideas like those gets stuck in people's minds, it's easy for them to start feeling like everything's better if we just stick to our own kind. People are scared of people who are different than them, they just are. And fear leads to hateful things like superiority, anger, and even violence. With colored folks having to stick to their own places, it makes it easier for white folks to go about their business unbothered."

Lily sat up straighter and stared hard at her father. She'd always loved listening to his voice, but he usually told her fairy tales or funny stories from the store or about his childhood. She didn't know he knew about all of this or even thought about it in any serious way. She felt quite grown up having this conversation.

"But what do *you* think, Daddy?" There it was; her moment of truth. Whatever Daddy, her hero, said next would have a profound impact on her young heart.

Daddy looked out at the water thoughtfully. "I think most colored folks are just as you said, people like us. They are fathers and mothers, shopkeepers and teachers. Now, to be sure, there are some bad eggs, but Lord knows white folks have plenty of bad eggs, too. Just the nature of our broken world. But I believe what the Bible says, and I believe that God calls us to love our neighbors as ourselves, and that means *all* our neighbors."

Lily exhaled. She'd been holding her breath, not wanting to miss a single syllable. "Is that why you took the sign off the front of the store? And why you sometimes give colored folk good deals on food?"

Daddy nodded. "You noticed that? My, Lily Jo, you are growing up right before my very eyes."

Lily beamed. "It's just... it feels like I'm learning a whole lot this summer, Daddy. But just so you know, I'm glad you do those things. It makes me real proud to be your daughter." She bit her lip, wanting to ask one him more thing, but unsure of how.

"Oh, I know that look, Lily Jo. What else is on your mind?"

"I know you don't agree with what Aunt Margaret said, but why didn't you say so?"

Daddy looked down at his hands. "Family is complicated, Lily Jo. We may not always agree, but we must always strive to get along. If I said something to Maggie, I'd be afraid that she'd hear it as an attack on her person. I'm afraid it might damage or even sever the relationship we have. People tend to cling tight to the things they've believed their whole lives. I'm not saying my fear makes it right, and I'm not saying I'll never speak with her about it in private. But the other day, with everyone there, was not the time."

Lily nodded. She thought she understood, but still an uneasy feeling settled inside her and she didn't know how to fight it. Who cared if Aunt Margaret got mad? Shouldn't she know she's wrong? Lily knew she'd never listen to her about it, but Daddy could help change her mind. If only he wanted to. Her face settled into a frown as she pondered this.

"Growing up can be a hard thing, Lily Jo. Now, what do you say we head back to dear ol' Maggie's before they send out a search party?" He ruffled Lily's hair, sending it into even more of a frizz than usual, and started rowing back to shore.

The food that night was delicious. Fresh fish and shrimp—caught by someone else, thankfully—cheesy grits, hush puppies fried to perfection, salty collard greens, all of Lily's favorites. Greta was no Maybelle, but she could cook a good meal. After everyone had stuffed their bellies, one by one they went inside to go to bed until only Lily and June were left on the porch, each holding a book in her hand. She could hear the mosquitos buzzing and was grateful for the screen.

"Hey June?"

"Yeah, Lil?"

"Do you think what Aunt Margaret said about colored folk is true?"

June was quiet for a long while, and Lily couldn't see her face. Then she simply said, "No."

"Daddy doesn't either, but he didn't tell her so."

June sat up from her swing and turned her body to face Lily. "You'll find out as you get older that some people are too stuck in their ways to change. Daddy probably feels like that about Aunt Margaret."

"Yeah. Still..."

"I know," June said quietly and turned back to her book.

Although Lily loved the Inlet, she was ready to go home. She missed Maybelle. And she missed Hazel. She wondered what Hazel had done with her long weekend and realized that beyond talking about her family, Lily didn't know much else about Hazel's life. They had spent a lot of time at Lily's, giggling about her own sisters or talking about the white side of Mayfield, but Hazel hadn't shared much about her home or school besides Miss Grace. She made up her mind to ask Hazel more about her life when she got home.

20

HAZEL

Hazel enjoyed the long weekend. She read halfway through *The Secret Garden* and couldn't wait to ask Lily how she liked the book so far. Hazel spent most of Saturday morning with Glory, walking the neighborhood in search of treasures like they had when they were younger and read together under Hazel's tree.

Saturday evening, she went to Wagner's Market with her mother. Walking through the store next to her, Hazel realized how much she had missed spending the long summer days with Mama.

"Are you havin' a good summer?" Mama asked.

"Yes, Mama! It's been good being at the Wagners'. Different than I expected."

"Well I'm glad. You sure been reading a lot."

"Yes!" She lowered her voice, looking around to make sure no one could hear her. "Lily's been letting me borrow books she likes."

"Oh, yeah? What's she like?" Mama asked.

"She's funny, Mama. She does and says whatever comes

into her mind and she's got these bright red curls that bounce when she laughs. And she laughs a lot. She's a good friend."

Mama smiled at the news. "I always thought you were much too serious, Hazel-girl. You had to grow up too fast. I know it's my fault, making you work and take care of the others. But I'm sure glad to see you having a taste of childhood now."

"It's been fun, though I wish being friends with Lily wasn't only possible because I gotta help Ma, you know?"

"I know, baby," Mama said. They walked in silence for a bit. Then Mama added, "You know, I'm not much of a reader myself, but I love that fire in your eyes when you talk about your books. I'm right proud of how hard you work in school too, Hazel. I got a feeling you gonna go far. Much farther than me or your Papa ever did in school," she said with a smile.

Hazel wrapped her arms around Mama's waist as they walked up to the meat counter.

When they got in line, Hazel spotted Mrs. Shaw and Hetty. Mama, of course, had heard all about Ma Maybelle and Hazel's visit and had seemed interested in meeting the white lady who let a colored girl live in her home as a resident rather than an employee. Hazel caught Hetty's eye and gave her a shy smile. Hetty's face lit up and she came over to them.

"Well hello, Hazel! How are you today?"

"Hi, Miss Hetty. We are doing all right. This is my mama," she said.

"Estelle Jackson," Mama said. "Nice to meet you."

"It's so nice to meet *you!*" Hetty said brightly. "Hazel is a real special girl. Miss Grace has told me a lot about her, and I enjoyed our conversation the other afternoon!"

Hetty introduced both Hazel and Mama to Mrs. Shaw, who smiled and said to Hazel, "My favorite delivery girl is out of town, so I had to come in for myself, but I guess you knew that!"

Mama's arm tightened around Hazel's shoulder, tense. Hazel knew it was because Mrs. Shaw was a white lady, but still it startled her to realize that her confident mother was nervous. Even in this nice store, Mama didn't feel completely safe.

Mrs. Shaw started to say something to Mama when Hazel heard a grunting, scoffing noise. Mr. Adams, Lily's surly neighbor, was scowling at their small group. He shook his head at Mrs. Shaw, clearly disappointed. Mrs. Shaw, not missing his mood, smiled brightly at him and said, "Good evening, Mr. Adams! They're having an excellent sale on whole chickens today!"

Mr. Adams, caught off guard, mumbled something Hazel was grateful she couldn't hear, and wandered off toward the produce section.

Mrs. Shaw turned her attention back to Mama and asked about her work and how she liked Mayfield. Mama answered her questions, tight-lipped but politely, until Hazel spoke up. "Mama's job at the hotel is hard. It leaves her and my sister Glory so tired. The owners don't give them a single break all day." Mama shot Hazel a look, one that meant she was in a heap of trouble. Hazel had no idea where her boldness had come from. She suspected, though, that Lily and her loud mouth had a little to do with it.

Mama's experience with white folks was so different from Hazel's that she must have expected Mrs. Shaw to prickle, look down at her, and ask coldly why she was ungrateful to have work at all. To Mama's clear surprise, however, Mrs. Shaw softened and said, "Well now, that isn't right. There has to be a law about that, right? A person can't work all those hours straight! The hotel you say? Hmm... I know the owners over there..." and her voice trickled off like she was forming a plan.

"Please, ma'am." Mama said so intently Hazel felt the

worry in her voice. "Please don't say nothing, I can't lose my job. I got mouths to feed."

Startled, Mrs. Shaw lowered her eyes and her voice. "Of course, I'm so sorry. I didn't mean to worry you. It just doesn't seem fair."

"Fair or not, ma'am, it's work, and I need it."

Mrs. Shaw's meat order came up, and Hetty went to the counter to collect it.

"I understand," Mrs. Shaw said, looking right into Mama's big brown eyes. She put her hand on Mama's arm and gave it a little pat. Mama's whole body froze, and Hazel knew why. She'd probably never in her life had a white lady touch her gently on purpose.

Hetty returned a moment later and gave Hazel a wink and a shining smile. "Mrs. Shaw, didn't you just lose your maid? Just a couple weeks ago?"

Hazel's heart clenched. *What was she doing?*

"Well, yes, I did," Mrs. Shaw answered, looking from Hetty back to Mama. "But I've been having the girls take cleaning shifts, to teach them a thing or two about keeping house."

Hetty went on. "When lessons start up again, Mrs. Shaw, will they—I mean, we—be able to keep up with it? It's an awfully big house."

Mrs. Shaw sighed. "You're probably right, Hetty. I'll probably have to find another maid soon."

Hetty looked at Hazel, who wasted no time. "My mama is a really good housekeeper, ma'am. And, she can cook almost as good as Ma Maybelle!"

Mama gave her a quick look like, *what you mean,* almost? but her face changed back to the worry it held before. Hazel bit her lip, but looked back to Mrs. Shaw, who had knit her eyebrows together.

All at once, Mrs. Shaw seemed to make up her mind about

something. "Can I ask you, Estelle, what the folks over at the hotel are paying you?"

Mama looked up, searching Mrs. Shaw's expression for any tinge of sarcasm or superiority, but finding none, she mumbled her wages.

"I'm sure we can do better than that," Mrs. Shaw said. "Come by the boarding house tomorrow after church and we'll talk. Only if you want, that is. I'll have the girls make us some tea."

"Okay." Mama's words came out slowly and carefully. "Thank you, ma'am," she said, her voice low, her eyes lower.

Hetty grinned at Hazel. "See you tomorrow, then!" she said before heading out the door.

Hazel looked up at Mama, who stood perfectly still, watching them leave. "I'm sorry for what I said about the hotel, Mama."

After what felt like an eternity, Mama said, "Oooh, baby girl, I was scared for a minute. I thought that white lady gonna go march up to the hotel and lose me my job! But instead..." her eyes searched the horizon, like she was dreaming of leaving the hotel. "Instead, you mighta just saved your mama. I wonder what Mrs. Shaw will have to say, 'bout Glory helping me."

"Only one way to find out."

ON SUNDAY AFTER CHURCH, Ma Maybelle started up a wild game of cards with Willie, Jr. and Tremaine was cheering on his brother when Mama, Hazel, and Glory headed over to the boarding house like Mrs. Shaw had asked. Hetty brought tea and cookies into the library for them and was overjoyed to meet Glory.

"You're sure blessed to have two smart and hardworking

girls!" Mrs. Shaw said as they all sat down. Though kindly spoken, the sentiment made Hazel wonder why it should seem extraordinary that colored children were smart or hardworking. Why should they have to work at all? Besides Lily's delivery service, she didn't know of any other jobs for white kids who lived in town.

"Now, Estelle," Mrs. Shaw continued. "What they're doing to you over at the hotel is not right. And I need a housekeeper here. I want to offer you the job, if you want it. It's a big house, but the girls keep it mostly tidy. And I'll leave it to you to manage yourself and rest when you need."

Mama was quiet for a moment. "What about Glory?" Mama asked, her voice shaking. "She's been working with me at the hotel."

"She's welcome to come on over here too. If Glory is anything like Hazel here, I'm sure she'll get along just fine."

"I don't know what to say, ma'am."

"Then say yes! I'd love it if you would," Mrs. Shaw replied.

In the end, they decided that Mama would give the hotel notice and start at Mrs. Shaw's the next week. She'd pay Mama and Glory five dollars a week more than the hotel. In addition to the cleaning, Mrs. Shaw had requested that Mama bake some of Ma Maybelle's famous breads and desserts for the girls once a week, but Mrs. Shaw would continue to do most of the cooking. She liked it, she said.

On the way out the door, Hazel whispered a "thank you" to Hetty, who just gave her a grin a shooed them out the door to enjoy the rest of their Sunday.

WHEN THEY GOT HOME, Ma Maybelle was playing dolls with Hallie and Nell, who were full of giggles and high-pitched squeals, making Ma smile. Willie Jr. and Tremaine had gone out and caught some catfish for their supper. Hazel told Ma to keep on with the little girls and she fixed dinner with Glory, leaving Mama to sit on the sofa with Papa's strong arm around her shoulder, watching their children with smiles on their face.

The rest of Hazel's family was excited to hear the news, and they celebrated with their big Sunday meal. Mama and Glory would be able to leave later in the morning and come home earlier in the evening. Papa was happy about the extra money, which meant that he could work fewer weekends and be home more often. They would have more time to spend together as a family. That night, Hazel's heart was as full as her belly.

21

LILY

After breakfast on Monday morning, Lily shouted a hasty, "Be back later!" to Hazel and Maybelle, ran out the door, and biked to the library. She had finished a couple of books at the Inlet and wanted to make sure Miss Nora counted them for the contest. Lily liked to get there when the doors first opened so she and Miss Nora could have a proper, uninterrupted conversation. She was disappointed, then, to see Beulah May Porter waiting on the steps of the library, her nose in a book. Beulah May didn't look up to acknowledge Lily's arrival, like she was ignoring her on purpose. Rolling her eyes, Lily pulled *The Secret Garden* out of her satchel and flipped to her bookmark.

She had come to a spot that was challenging. Normally, Lily read fast. So fast, in fact, that she missed important details and often had to retrace her steps to find missing information. However, she was struggling with this book because of the unfamiliar Yorkshire accents of a few of the characters. A lot of the time, she had to make her best guess of what the characters were saying. Once she figured out what the strange words meant, though, she picked up the pace.

Even though she knew people from different backgrounds often spoke differently, *The Secret Garden* made Lily wonder why the author wrote it that way. Midway through the story, she decided it was to show the difference between the wealthy, educated manor people and the poor country folk. And right there on the steps of the Mayfield Public Library, it occurred to Lily that although the Yorkshire of *The Secret Garden* was thousands of miles away and who knows how many years had passed since Dickon or Mary would've wandered the moors, there had always been a separation of people.

In Yorkshire, the line was drawn by the size of one's bank account, in Mayfield, by skin color.

The whole time Lily had been feeling confused about segregation, she'd failed to realize that beyond her own time and place, segregation had happened everywhere. Her father was right; it was how things always were. *But just because it's how things always were doesn't make it right,* she thought.

When Miss Nora finally pushed open the heavy doors, Lily emerged from the foggy moors of England and entered the familiar dustiness of the library. Beulah May got to Miss Nora's desk first and immediately started in on all that she'd read, heaving her large stack onto the circulation counter with a smirk in Lily's direction. Ignoring her, Lily set her bag down and wandered further into the library.

Lily sat down and read more of *The Secret Garden* until she saw Miss Nora and Beulah May marking the ledger. Beulah May had fifteen check marks by her name. Lily had only ten but had three more to add. Beulah May sneered at her and said, "Best of luck, Lillian."

Beulah May was the sort of person who did not believe in nicknames, asserting that a person's given name should be their name, no matter what that person preferred to be called. And, since the South was notorious for its nicknames—since it was much easier on the tongue to shorten just about every word—this particular personality quirk only added to Beulah May's unlikability.

Lily gave her best scowl back and fluttered her eyelashes with a sarcastic, "Why thank you ever so much, Beulah May."

Lily's mother, unlike Beulah May's, apparently, had not neglected to teach her basic Southern manners.

Beulah May stuck out her tongue and wandered away, looking for new books while Lily and Miss Nora talked about books for a while and marked her progress. No one had read nearly as many as the two girls, but she frowned when she saw Beau had six checkmarks next to his name.

Lily went to the stacks to look for more books to check out. Now, whenever she came to the library, she thought about Hazel and what she'd like to read, too. Hazel loved a good mystery, and Lily pulled a good-looking one from the shelf. She ended up with a stack of books larger than usual, some for her and some for Hazel.

Lily had decided that it was worth the risk of trouble to share library books with her friend. At first, she'd been worried that Miss Nora might notice, but she hadn't said anything so far. There were probably lots of folks who checked out books they never ended up reading.

Beulah May grunted loudly as she pulled down a heavy novel and added it to her large stack. She gave Lily another smug smile. Rolling her eyes, Lily decided to teach Beulah May a lesson.

She snuck over to the nonfiction section. Keeping one eye on Beulah May, Lily looked around for just the right thing. When she found it, she clapped a hand over her mouth so she wouldn't laugh out loud. She collected herself and strolled smoothly over to Miss Nora's desk where Beulah May's large stack sat, waiting to be checked out. Luckily, Beulah May had scampered off, saying, "Oh, just one more!" and luckily, Miss Nora had turned her back on the books for just enough time to let Lily slip another book into the middle.

Then, she found a nice chair within hearing distance of the desk and curled her legs under her, pretending to be deeply engrossed in the latest *Nancy Drew*. Eventually, Beulah May made it back to the desk and Miss Nora started working through her stack.

The kindly librarian froze when she picked up a small volume with a black cover. "Beulah May..." she said, pink rising to her cheeks. "I don't think *Womanhood and Marriage* is an appropriate book for you. There are... umm... just too many... umm... *adult* things in it. It's not quite for young ladies such as yourself."

Beulah May's face turned beet red, and she glanced around, making sure no one had heard. Lily kept her eyes firmly glued to her book, which she held very close to her face so no one could see her ear-to-ear grin.

"I... I... didn't want to check that out!" Beulah May said indignantly. "I promise! Where did you even get that, Miss Nora?"

"It was right here in your stack, the one you placed on the desk," Miss Nora said calmly.

"Then it must be a mistake! I would *never* read that!"

At this point, the back of Beulah May's neck and arms had turned bright red as well, and she was shaking.

Miss Nora tried to calm her down, but she seemed to just get more flustered instead.

"Oh, forget it! Put all of them back! I don't want any books today!" Beulah May shrieked, marching toward the door. When she passed Lily's chair, Lily gave her a wink and a smile.

Beulah May stopped, opened her mouth to say something but snapped it shut again, made a noise like that of an angry tomcat, and stormed off.

Lily couldn't help herself and laughed aloud, catching a stern look and a shush from Miss Nora. She couldn't wait to tell Hazel.

When she had checked out her own books, Lily said goodbye to Miss Nora and headed out the door. Walking out of the library, she passed two women pushing small babies in strollers, chatting away. Lily immediately recognized Mrs. Bell, who used to be Miss King, her third-grade teacher, but Mrs. Bell did not see her.

"Next thing you know, they'll be letting coloreds in here, you know," Mrs. Bell's companion said, scrunching up her face like she had tasted something sour.

Lily slowed to hear Mrs. Bell's response. Mrs. Bell had been a teacher, a kind one, a respected voice of authority in her own life, but Lily suddenly realized she had no idea how Mrs. Bell would respond.

"Oh, let's hope not, Rayanne, that would simply not do. Where would we take our children then?"

Lily sped up, her good mood about her prank on Beulah May disappearing as a deep disappointment settled in its place. She just couldn't understand the hatred that seemed to be present in every corner of Mayfield.

WHEN LILY GOT BACK to the house, Hazel wasn't there, and Maybelle was visibly upset and jittery. "Is everything all right?" Lily asked her.

"Oh, child, Hazel had to run on home. Tremaine's lungs. This heat ain't good for 'em. The neighbor called to tell us he's about to be in bad shape, so I sent Hazel to get his medicine from Doc Harding. He be okay when he can breathe again, Miss Lily, dontcha go on worrying."

"Is there anything I can do? Poor Tremaine. I bet Hazel's worried sick."

"She probably is, Miss Lily. Hazel's raised mosta those children like they her own. But she's a good girl. She'll get him all better soon."

Lily worried about Hazel anyway but didn't know how to help. She didn't have any money to give Hazel, and she felt a little nervous when she thought about running all over Hazel's colored neighborhood to try and find her.

Instead, she headed out to the porch to wait for Hazel. In her hurry, Hazel had dropped the notebook. Lily picked it up and settled herself on the swing to read Hazel's letter and wait for her return.

22

HAZEL

Hazel had been running ever since Ma Maybelle hung up the phone. When Tremaine started to show signs of troubled breathing, she only had thirty minutes before he'd be in serious trouble.

Hazel ran out of the Wagner house and all the way to the colored side of town. On her way, she passed the white drug store, which made her run faster, angry that she couldn't get what Tremaine needed there. Soon, she burst into Doc Harding's home where he saw patients and five minutes later, into her own house. There, she found quite a scene: Miss Essie was beside herself; Willie Jr. was not there, probably roaming the neighborhood unaware of the danger unfolding at home; and baby Nell was wailing. Hallie sat with Tremaine, stroking his back and whispering, "Shhh, brother, it's okay, shhh..."

Hazel rushed to Tremaine's side and with a shaky hand, gently coaxed him to take a spoonful of the thick liquid that smelled of eucalyptus and peppermint. He'd been wheezing badly, but after about ten minutes, his face relaxed, his skin felt less clammy, and his breathing became less labored.

Hazel exhaled.

He'd be okay.

She sat with Tremaine in her arms for a few minutes until he squirmed to get down to play.

Tearfully, Hazel thanked Miss Essie for calling her. Mama couldn't have left the hotel or she'd have been fired, and she didn't start at the boarding house for another week. Hazel gave Tremaine one last check-over, listened to his now free and clear breaths, and gave Miss Essie further instructions for his care.

"I've got to get back to Ma Maybelle, now, but he should be all right. Plus, Doc Harding said he'd be 'round to check on him after he was done with his next patient," Hazel said.

"Dear child, acting like a mother already, when you still a child yourself," Miss Essie said lovingly as Hazel turned to go.

Hallie followed Hazel almost all the way to the bus stop, clinging to her hand.

"Go on back now, Hallie-girl. Miss Essie needs you. And Tremaine needs you to be brave for him and sing him songs and tell him some stories, 'kay?"

"'Kay. Just come home soon, Hazel."

"I will, my love." She stooped to kiss the top of Hallie's head. "You did real good taking care of Tremaine."

HAZEL CAME BACK to the Wagner home drenched in sweat and breathing heavily. Lily got up out of her swing and quietly followed Hazel inside. When Hazel stepped into the foyer, she fell to the floor, put her hands on her face, and wept. All the adrenaline left her body and the reality of what had just happened hit her.

"He could've died," she sobbed.

Lily wrapped her arms around her friend's trembling body

and said, "Shhh, shhh. It's okay, you got there in time."

"But what if I hadn't? If only that old white doctor cared more about helping people than about what color their skin is, this wouldn't have even been so scary! I could've got what I needed right away, without running. I could've been there faster for him, to help him calm down sooner. It's not fair that doctor would rather let us die! Tremaine's a child! Just a child!" Hazel shouted, tears streaming down her face.

Lily didn't have a good answer for any of it, so she just sat next to Hazel, gently rubbing her back for a long while, until Hazel stopped shaking and was able to breathe again.

"I'm glad he's okay," Lily said softly.

"Me too," Hazel breathed. "But now I got a lotta work to do."

"C'mon," said Lily. "I'll help."

As they cleaned, Lily told Hazel all about Beulah May at the library, which cheered her up a bit. And then they talked about *The Secret Garden*.

"At first, though," Lily began, "I had a hard time reading their funny accents."

"Me too!" Hazel agreed, grinning. As they cleaned, they pretended to be Martha, one of Misslethwaite's many housemaids, and her brother Dickon. They both thought Dickon was the most likable boy they'd ever met, in literature or otherwise, and that young Colin was quite a strange fellow. Who would be happy spending their days in bed, ordering servants about and crying most of the time?

"Do you know much about gardening?" Hazel asked.

"Not a smidge!" Lily replied. "Daddy started one as a Victory Garden early in the war, but it's basically his fourth child. He doesn't want any help from us. How about you?"

"We grow a few things, mostly yams and greens. Plus a few things Ma Maybelle and Mama can for the winter. Ooh, you should hear Willie, Jr. complain about the weeds!" They both giggled. "But the way that Dickon breathed life into that dead garden was..."

"... Magical!" Lily finished.

"Yes, magical. And the way he talked to the animals. I've never seen a real person like that."

"Me either."

Before they knew it, the cleaning was done, and the girls sat side by side on Lily's floor, their knees curled up to their chests. Lily told Hazel all about the Inlet and Aunt Margaret's house and Alice the ghost. Hazel filled Lily in on Mama's new job that she'd start the next Monday. Lily clapped her hands with glee. "Your mama will love it there! I just know it!"

Hazel got quiet, then, and said, "Hey, Lily? You know in *The Secret Garden* how Dickon and Martha and the servants are poor? And how they live far off in a village away from the manor?"

"Yeah?"

Hazel took a deep breath and said slowly, "Did you notice that the wealthy folks in the story are the most miserable people you've ever seen? They have expensive furniture and grand hallways and delicious meals at the ring of a bell, but unhappiness seems to seep into their hearts like a poison." Lily nodded and Hazel continued. "But the servants are happy. They may not have much but they sure love the people they share it with."

Lily looked at her very seriously, and said, "You might be onto something. Just because folks have money doesn't mean they don't have problems."

Hazel considered this. She only knew of life with very little money, so she thought people with money must be much happier. But, she supposed, money couldn't fix everything. It couldn't save Mary Lennox's parents, after all.

The girls sat quietly for a bit longer.

Lily broke the silence. "Hazel? I wanted to come find you today, and help out with Tremaine. But I realized I'd never been over to the colored side of town. I wouldn't even know your house if I saw it. It's a bit strange, thinking that you spend your days here, but I don't even know where you lay your head at night. What's it like?"

And then Hazel told Lily all about her home, about the mattresses on the floor and the bedroom she shared with her sisters, how Ma Maybelle slept on a sofa. She told Lily about the peeling wallpaper and the water-stained ceiling and the window in the back that had a crack from top to bottom. How the front door hung crooked on its hinges and let the spring dust and winter cold inside. How they all shared one small bathroom. How the kitchen table wobbled and how some of the mismatched chairs had to seat two bottoms in order to fit the whole family.

But she shared, too, about all the love that kitchen held, all the nights they sat together as a family, holding hands and saying grace, all the jokes and laughter and hugs. Lily listened quietly, happy that Hazel had invited her into this corner of her life.

When Hazel stopped, Lily reached out and grabbed her hand. "Thank you for telling me. I'd love to visit your home sometime. I mean it," she added when Hazel looked at her skeptically. "I bet you think my house is ridiculous, right? The silver we barely use, things we've collected that we don't really care for?"

Hazel looked down. "I did at first. But not anymore. Now I see you folks as just living your lives, same as us. It's just our lives are different. And that's okay."

After a minute of quiet, Hazel said, "Hey! I know! You should come to our Wednesday evening prayer night at my church this week. We'll say a special one for Tremaine!"

"Would it be okay for me to be there?" she asked timidly.

"Of course! You'd be with me," Hazel assured her.

"Okay!" Lily agreed with a smile.

On Wednesday, Hazel waited for her friend on the steps of New Pilgrim Baptist Church. She stood when she saw Lily sprinting toward her on her delivery bike, red curls flying, pink cheeks. They were a couple minutes late, and almost every eye turned to watch the two of them walk through the door. Hazel looked around at her beloved church and tried to see it through Lily's eyes. She'd never seen the inside of the Methodist Church where the Wagners spent their Sunday mornings, but she imagined at the very least that it was newer and shinier than this.

The red carpet was stained and torn, the pews mismatched, the tapestries on the walls faded. The pulpit was unsturdy, wobbling as Reverend Moore animatedly shouted Bible verses at them. Hazel felt Lily stiffen next to her.

"Is he *angry?*" she whispered to Hazel, who giggled and shook her head. Once the congregation shouted back at him, "Amen!" and "Yes, suh!", Lily smiled and tried to join in when she could.

As soon as the choir started singing, Lily relaxed. Up there on the front row stood Ma Maybelle, right behind the Reverend, who had joined the choir and was singing out with his usual deep baritone and fiery passion. Ma Maybelle caught Hazel's eye, even in the way back, and gave her a nod and a smile. Hazel wondered if it was unnerving for Lily to be the only white face in a sea of dark. She knew how she felt every time she went to the white side of town.

Ma Maybelle happened to sing a solo that night, one she

often sang in the kitchen as she worked, one that always brought Hazel a sense of calm. She looked over and found Lily joining in the singing, too, "It is well, it is well, with my soul."

After folks shared problems and others laid hands on them in prayer, including Tremaine, Reverend Moore announced that it was time to take up the offering. Lily, surprised when an usher handed her the plate, threw in a nickel. The usher smiled at her, nodding his head as he took the plate.

"One more thing," Reverend Moore said before the choir sang again. "Y'all might know that one of our brothers, a Mr. Joe Wallace of Charleston, is taking his voter suppression case all the way to the state Supreme Court."

Someone up front yelled, "Be near, Lord Jesus!"

"Mr. Wallace could sure use our help. I'll have the ushers pass around a petition to sign to show our support. Feel free to sign it as you feel led to."

Hazel's heart swelled, knowing that her church was playing a part in making things right. And it swelled even more when Lily reached out and squeezed her hand, a big smile on her face.

So many folks signed the petition that the papers didn't even make it to Hazel and Lily by the time the last song ended and Hazel guided Lily to the door. On the way out, the preacher shook both of their hands and said, "Mighty glad to have you here tonight."

Once they were out on the sidewalk, Lily said, "It's late, I need to get home."

"I'll walk with you to the big tree," Hazel said. "And, Lily? Thanks for coming with me tonight."

"Oh, I'm so glad I did! And you know something? Your church is fun! At my church, everyone's so stiff and quiet." Lily mimicked the congregation at her own church, and Hazel giggled.

23

LILY
AUGUST 1945

My dearest Hazel,

Oh, how I loved the ending of The Secret Garden*! I don't
think I'll ever forget the children's idea of Magic, how if you
believe in something enough, you can do it. Isn't that
wonderful? Anne would love that kind of Magic. With her
imagination, think of what she could do!*

*What I will forever keep in my heart from this story is the
idea that what happens inside you affects your outer
appearance. At the beginning, Mary and Colin both had pale
yellow skin, scraggily hair, and frowned constantly. But once
they began to spend time in the garden and experience joy
and friendship and belonging, their outside looks improved.
Lots of folks around here could use that lesson. I especially
loved this: "Where you tend a rose, my lad, a thistle cannot
grow." If you're a rose on the inside, bright and cheerful, then
nothing can turn you sour. It gave me such hope that people
can change. Every single character benefitted from knowing
Mary and from her determination to get into that garden.
Everyone except Dickon that is, as he was always a happy*

*fellow. Perhaps it was he who changed them all for the better.
What do you think?*

*Ooooh, I just loved it! I wonder what Mrs. Shaw will give
us next?*

Yours sincerely,
Lily

As soon as Lily signed her name with a little heart, she sat
down with a satisfied *plop* onto her bed. She'd been so
busy with grocery deliveries that she hadn't had much time to
talk to Hazel, but she was glad they could still write. *The Secret
Garden* was Lily's new favorite; she wasn't sure she'd ever find
another book as wonderful. Looking out the window, she could
see across to Main Street. Mornings usually weren't very busy:
a few cars, a few folks walking up and down, ducking into
shops.

Lily sighed. She did love Mayfield, after all, even though it
wasn't perfect.

But her smile faded into a pensive frown when she remembered what Hazel had asked her the day before.

"I've enjoyed these books, Lily. But I have to wonder: why
are all these books about white girls? Where are books about
girls like me?"

Lily had no answer. And honestly, before she met Hazel,
she'd never given it a single thought. The books Lily read in
school and at home had always been about white girls and boys.

Now that Lily thought about it, why shouldn't Hazel have
the chance to read about girls just like herself?

June poked her head in Lily's room, then. "Lily, I'm
heading to the library, do you want to come? I bet you have
some there in that stack to return."

Lily ignored her question, but said instead, "Hey June? You
ever notice all these books we read are only about white folk?"

June came all the way in the room and shut the door behind her and came and sat beside Lily. "Yeah, I've noticed that. Why are you asking? 'Cause you and Hazel have been reading together? Oh, don't give me that look, I know y'all have."

She nudged Lily with her elbow and gave her a kind smile. Ever since the night of the parade, Lily had been sharing more of these moments with June—grins and eyebrow raises at things they both found ridiculous. She was learning of a whole new side of June, and for the first time, she liked being around her eldest sister.

"Well fine, so I am. How come there aren't any books about colored folk?"

June held out a big library book for Lily to look at. She'd seen June reading it lately around the house, and it was *huge* so it had taken her longer than usual to get through it. Lily ran her fingers over the title, *Gone with the Wind* by Margaret Mitchell.

"This one has some colored folk in it," June went on. "But I don't think it's a real fair picture of them."

"Whaddya mean?"

"Well, for one, all the colored folk in here are slaves. And they're *happy* slaves. It's like Mrs. Mitchell wanted us to see slavery as something beneficial to colored folk. I just can't imagine there were that many happy slaves, can you?"

"I—don't suppose so. I guess I haven't thought about it much," Lily said quietly.

Maybelle's voice interrupted from downstairs. "Miss Lily, your daddy needs you to get down to the store!" After saying goodbye to June and stashing the notebook where she knew Hazel would find it, she scampered down the stairs and out the door.

Marty looked up from the meat counter when he heard the bells on the door welcome Lily into the busy store. He grinned.

"Big order for you today, Miss Lily! For Mrs. Shaw. I'm just finishing up the meat. It'll be ready in a jiffy!"

Lily said a quick, "Thanks!" and went to find Daddy. He was restocking the salt water taffy and handed one to his daughter. She unwrapped the wax paper and popped the sticky candy into her mouth, leaving her unable to speak for a few minutes.

"Mrs. Shaw hired Hazel's mama, to clean and do some cooking. But I bet you already knew that, didn't you?"

Lily nodded, her mouth still full, a smile dancing across her eyes. "I'm mighty glad she has a good place to work for someone who will appreciate her," Daddy went on.

"Mmmeeee toooo...," Lily mumbled.

"Say hello to her for me, will you? Her name's Estelle. Maybelle's star from heaven, she always says. And tell her that the bacon she likes is on sale this week!"

"Order's up!" yelled Marty, who walked toward Lily, his arms full of groceries. Lily kissed Daddy on the cheek and helped Marty load the bicycle.

───────

As Lily walked up to the wide porch of the boarding house, she spotted a dark face peeking out of the window. Before she could knock, the door opened and a girl not much younger than herself stood behind it.

"Lily?" the girl squealed.

"Glory?" Lily asked. She'd seen Hazel's sister from afar that night at church, but she'd also seen so many other folks, too. After one look at her dimpled smile, though, Lily knew it was her for sure.

"Yes!" Glory said. "Let me help you."

"It's so nice to finally meet you for real. Hazel's told me so much about you!"

Glory smiled shyly. "She told me lots about you too."

The girls walked into the kitchen and put things away. Hetty joined them and helped unload the bags.

"How's Miss Grace? Hazel just loves her," Lily said with a smile.

"She's really smart. I'm learning so much from her and I can see why Hazel enjoyed her class."

Hetty would make a great teacher, Lily could just tell. She spoke of learning and curiosity and books in a way that just sparkled out of her. Hetty made it seem like anything was possible if you were just willing to take chances and learn new things. Lily stole a glance at Glory, who was looking at Hetty with stars in her eyes, captivated.

After the bags had been emptied, Lily wandered down the hall to find Mrs. Shaw.

On her way, Lily spotted Hazel's mama. She was a younger Maybelle, with less exhaustion and fewer worry lines across her face. She was quite pretty and, Lily could tell, a kind but strict woman. *Kind of like Mrs. Shaw*, she thought, amused. Even though Lily knew who she was, if she'd met her on the street instead of here, she'd know this was Hazel's mama. They had the same golden eyes, the same long, skinny, graceful fingers, the same dimples. Hazel's mama gave Lily a tired smile as she approached.

"Miss Lily." Estelle held out her hand tentatively, like this wasn't something she did often.

"Yes ma'am. So nice to see you. Please just call me Lily, though, ma'am." Lily put her hand out as well.

The older woman took Lily's hand into both of hers then and looked Lily right in the eye. "Hazel's had a good time reading those books with you and sharing stories. I worry about her being lonely, y'know. She gotta act like such a grown up sometimes, but she been so happy this summer."

Lily smiled and said, "Hazel's so smart. And a great friend."

"Ain't she?"

Lily squeezed Estelle's hand. "Are you liking it here?"

"Yes, but I got lots to do. Glad to meet you, Lily." She let go of Lily's hand and turned back to her work, so Lily headed further into the house. As usual, she found Mrs. Shaw in the library, curled up with *Emma*, a thick Jane Austen novel.

She looked up as Lily entered and greeted her cheerfully. "How are you today, Lily?"

"Just fine," Lily replied. "Thank you so much for *The Secret Garden*." Lily handed her the book. "We both loved it. It was so magical and simple. I really liked how Mary Lennox started off as this spoiled, cranky, unlovable brat and ended up being a perfectly charming girl surrounded by friends and a new family."

"Ah, yes," Mrs. Shaw replied thoughtfully. "The best books of all have characters that do a lot of growing, don't they? Mary was the one who really made the garden come back to life. I love a good, unlikely heroine in a book! What shall you read next?"

Lily bit her lip. "Well, that's the thing. Hazel and I have enjoyed all the books you've given us, but..." she hesitated, unsure of how to form her next words. "We wondered if you had any books about colored folks? Especially colored girls? All the books at the library seem to be written by white writers about white folk."

Mrs. Shaw nodded gravely and looked down at her hands. "You see, Lily, this country is about as broken as Mayfield, in some ways more than others. A lot of publishers won't even consider books written by colored writers, so they are hard to find. I have read some poetry, but I don't own any. I'm sorry. Perhaps Hetty can help us."

Rose walked in and interrupted their conversation to tell Mrs. Shaw that the kitchen sink was leaking. Lily wished them both a good day and headed out the door, not wishing to be in the middle of a plumbing disaster.

The problem of not being able to find a book written by a colored person bothered Lily. She had, until then, operated under the assumption that although colored folks were separate, they still had all the things white folks did: restaurants, schools, doctors. Heat rose to her cheeks when she realized then that her assumption could not be true. After all, colored folks didn't even have a library. Hazel's papa and others like him weren't allowed to do a simple thing like vote. And now she learned they had a hard time getting published? Of course they did, why should she be surprised?

On her way home, Lily rode her bike past Jean's and saw Elsie and Francis from school. They were sharing a chocolate malt and had their heads together, giggling over something. Pangs of jealousy and then anger shot through Lily. She couldn't ever bring Hazel to Jean's to share a milkshake. Besides the restaurant's rule of whites only, Lily realized—surprising herself—that she couldn't bear to think of what people would say. Beau seeing them together was one thing, but the whole town was another matter. If they were angry that Mrs. Shaw took in Hetty, what would they say about her friendship with a colored girl? And wouldn't she be putting Hazel in some kind of danger, like June said after the parade? Lily felt shame rise up in her as she wondered why she even cared what people would think, how she could think of that before Hazel's well-being.

Why did life have to be so complicated?

Lily decided to go to the library and ask Miss Nora for a

book about colored folk. She sensed, perhaps instinctively, that there would be no point in looking at the Mayfield Library, but she thought she'd try anyway. Colored folks weren't even allowed in there; why would there be any books by them or for them? Did white folks in the South believe that colored people could not be as talented as they? That they could not tell stories as well? Lily personally knew this to be untrue—Maybelle's stories were unmatched. The thought made Lily's heart drop into her stomach. Still, she had to try, so she pushed open the doors of the library and stepped inside.

Miss Nora was busy talking with some of Lily's classmates and counting books for the contest, so Lily decided to have a look around instead. She didn't know where to start, so she walked over to the children's section first. Choosing a random shelf, she began examining picture books, studying their covers, flipping through the illustrations. After she'd looked through about twenty books and had found no evidence of colored children, she got up and found a different shelf, getting the same results as before. Lily glanced up at the circulation desk and noticed Miss Nora was finally alone.

"Miss Nora?" she asked, a bit shyly, which made Miss Nora look at her with almost a motherly concern. Lily was not usually shy or hesitant in this place.

"Why, Lily, you're awfully quiet today, is something the matter?"

Lily didn't know how much this meant to her until she felt a familiar lump in her throat. She cleared it before answering the librarian.

"Miss Nora, do you have any books about..." she lowered her voice and looked around to see if anyone was listening. "... colored folks?"

Miss Nora looked down at her hands and all the color left her cheeks. Matching the volume of Lily's voice, she replied,

"Well, your sister June just returned *Gone with the Wind*, but that's a mighty large book for a girl your age. There are others where families have colored maids or butlers or drivers. Would you like me to look for a few of those?"

"Oh. Um, no thank you, Miss Nora. I was more looking for a story about a colored girl, maybe my age? I was ... um... just wondering what life might be like for one, that's all."

"We don't, Lily. I'm afraid I don't have much choice in the matter."

Lily understood. The Mayfield Public Library got most of its money from the town government and Lily knew that Mayor Green was especially concerned with the town's appearance, with propriety, and with keeping old traditions alive.

"Do you know where I could find some?"

Miss Nora looked at her then. "The bigger cities might have a few, but Mayfield is just too small. I'm sorry, Lily."

"I understand. Thanks anyway, Miss Nora."

Miss Nora smiled at her sadly. "Do you have any books to add to your checklist?" she asked, trying to cheer Lily up.

Lily told her all about *The Secret Garden* and about a few others she had read. When they finished, Lily waved goodbye to Miss Nora, who said, "Take care, now." As she stepped into the sunlight, Lily's heart sank, realizing that she still hadn't found a book for Hazel.

Instead of going home, Lily rode her bike all over town, past downtown with its little shops and past City Hall and the courthouse. She rode past the Methodist Church her family attended every Sunday with lots of other white folks. She rode past the junior high school where she'd spend her days in just a few short weeks with only other white students. She rode all the way to the end of Main Street, where all she could see beyond the lonely stop sign were acres and acres of farmland, owned by mostly white folk but worked mostly by colored men.

The heat was stifling and Lily was soaked with sweat, so she stopped to admire the beauty of the green crops swaying in the breeze. She wished, just for a moment, that she could leave Mayfield and all the unfairness and ugliness behind and just run and run until she couldn't anymore.

But she didn't. Instead, Lily hopped off her bike and sat by the side of the road until the sun started to hang low in the day. Dusk was Lily's favorite time, when the air felt almost hazy, sleepy, a gentle warning that night would come soon and with it, a time of rest. Lightning bugs came out at dusk, and so did neighbors who had taken refuge from the heat inside during the day. One by one, the lights along Main Street flickered on and Lily pointed her bike toward home, so she'd make it in time for supper.

Maybelle and Hazel had already gone home for the evening, and Lily felt relieved. She knew she had to answer Hazel's question, but she didn't know how. Her only hope was that maybe Hetty could find something.

As Lily ate her supper quietly, a meal that Maybelle had prepared for her, she thought about how she had done nothing to deserve her comfortable life on the white side of town with a family who had found success and wealth. On the other hand, Hazel had done nothing to get where she was either. The only difference between them was the shade of their skin. Lily couldn't bear to think about any of it anymore. She went upstairs and fell fast asleep.

THE NEXT MORNING, Lily awoke slowly, the memory of yesterday's thoughts heavy on her heart. As usual, Marianne was still in bed, lightly snoring. Lily could smell something delicious in the kitchen, but was not ready to face the day. She groaned and threw one arm out of bed, hanging her head lazily over the side. Peeking out at her from between her mattresses like an old friend was the notebook.

Dear Lily,

I wasn't ready for The Secret Garden *to end. I do think Dickon brought out the best in Mary. His joy was contagious, and he taught Mary and Colin how to feel happiness. I thought a lot about Dickon's Magic, too. I wonder if the author meant that we all have magic inside us. Colin's problem was that before Mary Lennox, he didn't even want to try to get better, but once he had an idea of something better out there, it was much easier for him to walk. But I have to say, I think the writer might be a little too hopeful with the idea that we can change all things if we just believe enough. What about the things we can't change? No matter how hard we try? I guess what I'm saying is I liked the message of the Magic because it inspires hope, but also, it made me sad to know that I don't have the power to fix some things.*

I need to get back to work. I hope you know I still loved the book, even if it made me sad.

Until next time,

Hazel

24

HAZEL

Hazel didn't know how late Lily had come home the night before because she'd left a little early herself. The question she'd asked Lily had invaded her mind like an occupying army and refused to leave. So, she finished her work early, made sure Ma Maybelle could manage without her, and mumbled something about needing to get home. Ma shooed her out the door. Hazel knew Ma could tell she was fibbing. Maybe she wanted to give Hazel some time to enjoy the summer. But, instead of going home, Hazel made her way to the school and found Miss Grace's door standing wide open. She heard light-hearted laughter coming from the classroom and grinned when she saw Hetty inside.

"Hazel! Come in! How are you?" Hetty asked.

"Pretty good. How are you both?"

"Well, we're supposed to be working," Miss Grace said, "but I just got to telling Hetty about the time I caught ol' Johnboy Lewis with a frog in his underpants, no doubt a schoolboy prank gone awry."

Hazel laughed, remembering the day well.

Then she got right to it. "Miss Grace," she started, "Lily and I finished *The Secret Garden,* my favorite book of the summer so far. But... it got me to thinking. All these books are about white girls. Where are the books about us?"

Miss Grace shot a meaningful look at Hetty, teacher speak for *this is an important moment, so pay attention.*

"Oh, Hazel," Miss Grace began. "Most of the literature I've read by colored folk is poetry or memoirs, some of which I've shared with my students, but oftentimes, colored folk write about slavery, or abolishing it, or life as a freeman in the South with Jim Crow. And while I do want my students to know the truth, some of it's not right for young minds to hear just yet. I have yet to find a book written by a colored writer just for children."

Hazel nodded. She understood. There were certain adult things she didn't particularly want to think about until she had to. "But what about white writers? Do none of them write about colored folk?"

"The few books I've read like that included colored folk as side characters, and honestly, most of them made colored folk out to look plain lazy, or ignorant, or the cause of any trouble in their parts. Books like this aren't fair; they make white folk think we're all the same as those characters, and it just isn't the truth."

Hazel looked down at her dusty toes, peeking out of her worn sandals. She had guessed as much, but she knew if anyone could give her an answer, Miss Grace could.

"I understand. I'll let you get back to work now. Thanks anyway..." she started, and turned to leave, but Miss Grace put a hand on her arm.

"Wait. I know it's not a book, but I might have something for you." Hazel's gaze lifted and met Miss Grace's, her eyes shining like they held a great secret.

She pulled out what looked like an old magazine from her top desk drawer and handed it to Hazel, who recognized the cover from when Miss Grace read aloud to the class. The title said *The Brownies' Book* and when Hazel gently flipped it open, she saw that it was full of poems, essays, and even a few puzzles. It was different from any magazine she'd ever seen, which had mostly been Marianne's fashion magazines that were always strewn about her room. The bright pages in those magazines showed tall, white, blonde models in photographs or illustrations. The yellowed pages of *The Brownies' Book*, though, were printed on less expensive paper, less durable. The ink was smudged in a few places; it had obviously been read a few times.

"It's a literary magazine," Miss Grace explained. "The publishers, editors, and writers were all colored, like us, and it was created specifically for colored children. They only published it for two years, from 1920-1921, so there weren't that many issues. I'm lucky to have the ones I do."

Hazel glanced up. "How'd you find these?"

Miss Grace looked at Hazel, her eyes still sparkling. "A friend from up North sent them. Here in South Carolina, it would've been hard to get them. Postage is expensive, and townspeople wouldn't look too kindly on it. I'd love to get copies for the whole class to read, but I could never do that. So, I read aloud from them instead. Here, you take this one. Just... Hazel?"

"Yes'm?"

"Be careful where you read it. There's lots of white folks who'd frown on you reading something like this, even though they wouldn't know what's inside, or even take the time to find out."

Hazel nodded. "Thank you, Miss Grace. I'll bring it back when I'm finished." She paused. "Can I show it to Lily?"

Miss Grace raised an eyebrow at Hetty, who put a warm hand on Hazel's and said gently, "She's your friend."

Miss Grace nodded in agreement, and Hazel tucked the magazine into her bag carefully, feeling like a smuggler of great treasure.

―――――――

THAT NIGHT, Hazel flipped through *The Brownies' Book*, taking care with its fragile pages. For Lily's sake, she did not stop to read any of the featured articles. She wanted to save those to read together.

The cover was simple; the title ran across the top and underneath it were two photos of a young girl, maybe six years old, with short curly hair, and skin the color of Hazel's. In one picture, the girl looked down and to the side, like she was deep in thought. In the other, she looked up, hopeful, happy. The girl reminded Hazel a bit of sweet little Hallie, snoring away in the next room right in the middle of a pile of children.

Hazel eyed the table of contents, full of stories and poems that she couldn't wait to read. There were photos of groups of young colored people and individual photos of babies and young children titled "Our Little Friends" and "Little People of the Month." Beautiful illustrations and designs livened up the pages with longer stories, and Hazel loved that they were all done by colored artists.

Although this was the hottest summer she could remember living through, Hazel's arms were covered in goosebumps. *The Brownies' Book* suddenly felt heavy, as if it carried great significance. She'd never seen a collection of writing completely dedicated to colored folks, celebrating them, printing their words. Hazel imagined the thrill of having her own words published someday, how she'd glow with pride seeing her name in print.

But why had the magazine gone out of print after just two years? Had something happened to the publisher? Was it a money problem? Hazel knew that 1921 was well before the big stock market crash that had caused so many difficulties. Whatever the reason, she was grateful to have the April 1921 issue in her possession.

As she thumbed through the pages, she realized that the children in the photos would now be all grown up, that they had lived through the Great Depression and the war as adults. How had they fared?

With a shiver, Hazel wondered how many had lived.

Hazel thought back to what Miss Grace had taught her class about the Depression. That even white families had a rough time. But that poor folks became even poorer. Most colored folks Hazel knew were already poor, so she could imagine how it had only gotten worse for them. Miss Grace had shown photographs of the shacks and shanties where people had been forced to live, of the lines they had formed to wait for food, their tattered clothes hanging limply from emaciated bodies and their hollow cheekbones unable to muster even the slightest suggestion of a smile for a photographer.

No, the smiling folks in *The Brownies' Book* had not been through the hardest of times yet. It made Hazel sad to think of them, taking photographs, starring in plays, writing fantasy stories, not knowing what tomorrow would bring. But too, she was glad that they'd gotten to live with such joy.

———

LILY DIDN'T COME downstairs until Ma Maybelle and Hazel had cleaned up after breakfast, which was unlike her. When she finally came down the stairs, her head hung low and she walked slower than usual, her feet weighed down by some invisible force. Giving Hazel a sad smile, she slumped down at the kitchen table and rested her head on her arms. Ma Maybelle gave Hazel a sideways look and raised an eyebrow before pushing a plate of eggs and bacon and a still-warm biscuit dripping with sweet grape jelly toward Lily. Then she left the kitchen.

Hazel sat down next to her friend and put a hand on her shoulder. "What's wrong?"

Lily sighed loudly and covered her eyes. "Oh, Hazel. It's just awful. I've completely failed you."

"What do you mean?" Hazel asked, eyes wide.

"I couldn't find a book for us, Hazel. You know, about..." she lowered her voice, "a colored girl like you. Mrs. Shaw has none, the library has none. I don't know where else to look!" Lily said, letting out another loud sigh and putting her head back down, unable to look Hazel in the eye.

Hazel couldn't help but laugh. She could picture Lily riding all over town, pedaling frantically, red curls blowing around her face, on a search for a book, of all things. Lily looked up, confused by Hazel's laughter. "Oh, Lily. Thanks for trying. I mean it. But yesterday I went over to Miss Grace's. She told me that it's real hard for small towns in the South, especially South Carolina, to get books like that," Hazel explained.

"Mrs. Shaw said the same thing. But oh, Hazel, how can you laugh? It's just dreadful."

"It is sad. And it isn't right. But really, I'm not all that surprised. Plus, Miss Grace gave me something else. Wait here."

Hazel left the kitchen and returned in a jiffy with *The Brownies' Book*. She held it out to Lily, whose face changed from utter despair to pure delight. She squealed and reached out tentatively to touch it.

Hazel explained what it was, giving her all the information

Miss Grace had given her. "I gotta give it back to her, though," Hazel added. "They're not in print anymore, and Miss Grace treasures them."

Lily finished her breakfast and cleaned up after herself. Ma Maybelle came back in the kitchen to prepare supper, and she shooed the girls out. Lily helped Hazel clean, and once the beds were made and the furniture polished, the girls sat side by side on Lily's bed.

Hazel read the first story aloud: "How Br'er Possum Outwitted Br'er Rabbit" by Julian Eliha Bagley. It was a folk tale told by a grandmother whose cheeky grandson had bamboozled her into story time so he could escape his homework. The girls chuckled, both familiar with the Br'er Rabbit tales.

In the next article, Langston Hughes described the city in Mexico where he lived. Hazel and Lily both usually preferred fictional stories, but the way Mr. Hughes described Toluca was fascinating. Lily read it aloud slowly, so they could savor the details, pausing to close their eyes tight and use Hughes' words to take them far away. The details were so vibrant and real, they could almost see the mountains looming in the distance, smell the rain on rich soil, taste the mangoes and peppers. As they gazed at an illustration of villagers, some carrying food on their heads and others caring for children, they agreed that life in Toluca was very different from life in Mayfield.

Lily and Hazel had just peeked at the next page, which was full of brain teasers and logic puzzles, when they heard Ma Maybelle hollering for help. Hazel looked at Lily and shrugged. "Tomorrow?" she asked.

"Tomorrow," Lily replied. "I oughta get to the store anyway and check on Daddy." Lily handed *The Brownies' Book* back to Hazel, who tucked it safely into her bag, and they headed their separate ways.

HAZEL SPENT the next morning cleaning and setting up the
Wagner home for one of Mrs. Wagner's bridge club luncheons.
When Mrs. Wagner had explained to Ma and Hazel what she
expected for the luncheon, Hazel had noticed that Ma's lips
were pressed in a firm line the entire time. When she'd asked
Ma about it later, she'd complained about her knees hurting
her, and she told Hazel that these bridge luncheons were a lot
of work and that everything had to be absolutely perfect. They
were some of Ma's least favorite days working for the Wagners.

Hazel soon found out why. The work involved moving
heavy furniture to make room for folding tables covered in
white lace tablecloths and surrounded by four chairs each.
Hazel set each place with a silk napkin, three different forks, a
spoon to stir the iced tea and another one for dessert, and two
knives, one to butter rolls and another to slice the roasted
chicken Ma Maybelle was preparing. She had to check and
double-check the placement of the silverware; Mrs. Wagner
had been clear that no piece should be out of place.

Lily spent the morning delivering groceries, so when she
returned around noon, she and Hazel were both sweaty and
tired. The bridge ladies arrived soon after. Mrs. Wagner
greeted her guests wearing a pale blue dress that flattered her
slight figure. Hazel and Lily took the ladies to their seats and
served each course, carrying plates to and from the kitchen. Ma
Maybelle had done this so many times she was as calm as ever,
handing the girls dishes that she'd already plated.

At last, they served the floating island dessert, a favorite of
Mrs. Wagner's, a heaping dollop of meringue atop a scoop of
warm custard. Hazel and Lily were delirious from the heat and
the rushing back and forth. While the ladies ate, the girls
washed and dried the fragile china as well as the pots and pans

as soon as Ma finished using them. She must have recognized their exhaustion because she thanked them for their help before hustling them out of the kitchen.

"I'll get the dessert plates. Y'all go on and do whatever it is you do. Them ladies'll be playing bridge for hours, just make sure y'all ain't making no racket."

"Yes ma'am," they said in unison. Hazel wasn't sure why Maybelle had been so concerned about *them* making noise, because those refined women sure whooped it up, gossiping and celebrating the end of an exciting hand of bridge.

"C'mon," Lily said. "Let's go read *The Brownies' Book* on the porch. I'll show you my favorite spot. The breeze hits it just right. It's too warm inside."

Hazel bit her lip. "What if someone sees?"

"Oh, it's the middle of the day and all the mothers are inside our very house and not likely to come out for a bit. It'll be okay," Lily replied, waving away Hazel's worry. Hazel frowned, thinking back to the night of the parade and Beau, but she didn't say anything.

Three minutes later, they were sipping sweet tea on the two-seater swing, and Lily was reading aloud from an article called "Girls Together." In it, they learned of a young girl named Sarah Grimke from South Carolina who'd lived before the Civil War. Her family had owned slaves on their rice plantation, but Sarah grew to hate the institution of slavery. She taught her own personal slave—a gift from her father—how to read, knowing full well that teaching a slave to read was against the law. Sarah went on to be a well-known abolitionist, someone who spoke out against slavery and worked to end the practice in the United States.

Lily stopped reading and set the magazine down.

"What in the world?" she asked. "How could teaching someone to read be a crime?" She looked sadly at Hazel. "They didn't teach us about this part of slavery in school. Our books said slaves were mostly well taken care of by their masters. That the plantations gave them food and safe places to sleep. This just said some slaves got whipped for bad behavior. I wonder what else my books left out."

Hazel looked down at her hands. "I know what your books say. Because we always get the old ones your school doesn't want anymore. But Miss Grace told us other things, read us some parts of an escaped slave's autobiography, one who was lucky enough to learn to read and write." She lowered her voice to just above a whisper. "Slaves were taken from Africa in chains and put on boats where many of them got very sick or died on the way to America. Then, they got sold away from their families, like Ma Maybelle's mama. Lots of them were beaten every day, and many were even killed."

Lily was clearly horrified; her eyes were wide and she'd clapped a hand on one cheek. "But... why?"

They were so deep in their conversation that they didn't hear the heavy footsteps coming up the porch, and the next minute, Mr. Adams appeared, wearing an angry grimace. "Because," he snarled at them, "Negroes were made to be slaves, made to serve white men, who are superior to coloreds in every way."

Hazel and Lily froze. There was nowhere to hide *The Brownies' Book*. He'd already seen it. They watched in horror as Mr. Adams snatched it from Lily's hands.

"What is this *filth*?" he yelled. "What would your daddy think about you reading such trash, young lady? And with a *Negro*?" He spat out the word "Negro" like it was a piece of rotten meat.

Hazel stole a look at his face for just a moment. Mr. Adams was red all over, his brow furrowed, and his nose scrunched up in anger, showing every one of his teeth like a rabid wild animal. Neither girl said a word, hoping that Mrs. Wagner would come outside to investigate the shouting, but Hazel could hear the ladies chattering away inside as they changed tables.

Hazel winced when she heard Mr. Adams flip through the pages of *The Brownies' Book*, but she dared not look at him again. Mr. Adams grew more and more furious as the seconds ticked by. He shook in a full rage when he finally closed the magazine and got right up in front of Lily, wagging a tobacco-stained finger in her face.

"You listen to me girl. This book is full of lies. Full of trash. I guarantee that even your daddy, the *honorable* Mr. Wagner, would not like you reading this. Especially with *her*," he spat again, this time in Hazel's general direction.

"In fact," he sneered, his face so close that Hazel could smell stale cigarettes on his breath. "I'm gonna take this down to his store right now and tell him what you're doing." He grabbed Lily's arm, hard, and lowered his voice to a deep growl, "Oh, now wait a minute. You're not friends with this Negro, are you?"

Lily stayed silent just a bit too long for Mr. Adams, infuriating him even more. He grabbed her other arm and shook her violently. "Well? I asked you a question!"

Lily looked at Hazel, pain and fear in her eyes, and then looked down at her feet. When she looked up again, though, she had a wild look about her that frightened Hazel.

"She's a good person, sir." Lily answered, her voice trembling. "And her and Maybelle are the best help we ever had!" She snuck Hazel a small, panicked smile like she was doing her some kind of favor, in defending her honor to this horrible man.

"Then y'oughta treat her more like the help, for God's sake," Mr. Adams growled. He released Lily's arm and walked away from the house with great purpose in his steps, gripping

The Brownies' Book so tightly Hazel thought it might disintegrate.

Neither girl spoke. Lily—too late—realized what she'd said, and looked at Hazel with wide, sad eyes. "I didn't mea—" but Hazel could not listen to the rest. Surely she didn't just call her "the help."

Surely.

Anger burned Hazel's cheeks and tears stung her eyes. She'd never been so scared in all her life, but with the immediate threat of Mr. Adams gone, a new feeling took its place.

Betrayal.

Lily, her friend. The one she'd shared stories with, talked about important things with, and laughed with, had called Hazel "the help." Even if she'd tried to stand up for Hazel's character, the dismissal of the friendship they'd built was too much to bear. And besides, Hazel didn't need anyone to defend her character, she showed folks she was a good person everyday by her actions. It was as if a dam broke then, and Hazel said quietly, through silent tears, "How could you, Lily?"

"I just thought... I didn't... oh, Hazel," Lily stumbled, not knowing what to say.

"No, you didn't think," Hazel said icily. "You never do."

Without looking at her friend, she quietly slipped around back to the kitchen, avoided Ma Maybelle's eyes, and told her she didn't feel well and needed to go home. She ran the whole way there, her muscles burning with the kind of pain that now settled her heart.

———

Later, as she sat under her oak tree with nothing but the heat of the day and a lone squirrel for company, she realized that deep down, she knew Lily didn't mean it. She couldn't. Unless she'd been the world's worst liar every day since the first time she'd seen Hazel's journal. No, she'd been scared. Hazel had been frightened, too. Even so, hearing the words escape from Lily's lips was so much worse than Hazel could have ever imagined.

25

LILY

L ily sat frozen on the porch until she saw Hazel's small form moving quickly down the sidewalk away from the house. At the sight of her braids swinging, Lily burst into tears, ignored the bridge ladies as she ran up the stairs, and didn't stop crying until she heard the door creak open slowly. In the next moment, she felt her daddy's strong hand on her shoulder.

"Oh, my sweet Lily Jo," he started.

She couldn't look at him. Shame threatened to come up and burst out of her. "I don't know the details of what happened today, but I have a pretty good idea. And I'm so sorry, darlin'. Mr. Adams should never have yelled at the two of you like that. He was wrong, and I told him as much when he came flying into the store. I can't imagine how frightened you must have been."

Lily sighed, heavy with grief and guilt. "That... wasn't... even... the... worst... part... Daddy," she managed, her words punctuated by heaving sobs.

"What do you mean?"

Her breathing calmed and she replied, "I told Mr. Adams that Hazel was just 'the help'. Right in front of her."

Daddy was quiet for a minute, then picked Lily up and cradled her like he'd done when she was much smaller. Looking right into her eyes, he said, "Now Lily Jo, you were scared. We all do things differently when we're scared. Hazel knows you didn't mean it, darlin'."

"But Daddy... I said it. I'm afraid that's all that matters," she cried, burying her face into his shirt. He didn't say anything else. He just held her until the light in the room faded and it was time for supper

"It'll be okay, Lily Jo, you'll see," he said in a strong, confident voice. "And," he added, "you can give this back to Hazel."

He handed *The Brownies' Book* to Lily. By some miracle it had survived Mr. Adams's rage; it looked no worse for wear. She hugged the magazine to her chest.

"Oh, thank you, Daddy!"

THE NEXT DAY, Hazel did not come to Lily's house with Maybelle, which pushed Lily farther down into her pit of grief. Maybelle gave Lily a sad sort of smile, but when Lily sobbed out a "I'm so sorry, Maybelle," she pulled Lily into one of her warm bear hugs.

"Shh, now, Miss Lily, things gon' work out. Hazel's hurt, you know that. And it may take her some time to trust you again. My Hazel's a cautious girl, real smart and kind, but cautious. And rightly so. Give her some time. And make sure you tell her you're sorry. Apologies may be hard to say, but they some of the most important words you can ever utter. 'Specially when you know you done something wrong." Her words made Lily's tears come again, and they threatened to never stop.

As Maybelle fried an egg for Lily's breakfast, she said, "It was wrong of that man to attack two little girls. Wrong, ya hear? It ain't none of his bisness whatchu do with your time. He ain't your daddy. He wrong, Miss Lily, and I'm telling you the same thing I done told my Hazel last night. Ain't nothin' wrong with you two being friends or reading out there on that porch."

Lily wished with all her might that she could believe her.

Hazel didn't come the next day either and to Lily's surprise, she felt relieved. She didn't know how she'd face Hazel, what she'd say. That night, she pressed *The Brownies' Book* into Maybelle's hands and said, "I wanted to give this to her myself, but can you? I know Miss Grace wants it back."

DADDY, perhaps sensing that a little sea air would do everyone good, took them to the Inlet for another long weekend. Although Lily was happy to be near the water again, the visit was clouded by her deep sadness. And she wasn't sure she could bear any more talk of colored folk from Aunt Margaret, not with what had happened with Hazel. Luckily, they managed to avoid the topic in conversation altogether.

The weather mirrored Lily's mood; it rained for two straight days. Gray clouds sat on the water like unwelcome guests. At night, the Wagners sat on the porch and watched the rain fall in sheets from a darkened sky and listened to the pitter-patter of water on the metal roof. Aunt Margaret's weeping willow looked even sadder than usual, its wet branches heavy and burdened, a feeling Lily was sure she now understood.

Lily spent a great deal of time reading and sleeping in her little attic room. The sun came out the last afternoon and June and Marianne, taking pity on their little sister's broken heart, knocked on Lily's door.

"Oh, Lily, you must stop feeling sorry for yourself," Marianne started. "It's probably for the best, you know. You and that girl were going to get found out sometime, and you're lucky it didn't end up worse. It's just better for us to stick to our own kind, surely you can see that now?"

Lily, knowing full well how shallow and uncaring Marianne could be, wasn't exactly surprised but couldn't say a word.

"Oh, shut up, Marianne," June said harshly. "That's not helping. Just go find your friends or something."

Marianne shrugged her shoulders, like she was saying, *what did I do?* But then spat out, "Whatever," flipped her hair, and walked out the door.

"Thanks, Junie," Lily said, using a nickname from long, long ago. June sat down on Lily's bed and put an arm around her shoulders. "Marianne was right about one thing, though, and that's that you can't wallow in your sorrow. You'll need to find a way to say you're sorry, but until you can, it's not helping anybody to sulk around. Come on, let's go to Mo's. I think I saw some girls from your school there. They have that swirl ice cream cone you like so much."

"'Kay, fine," Lily responded sadly, and followed her sister down the stairs.

The fresh air and sunshine felt good on Lily's skin, and the knot that had formed in her chest started to unravel.

Sure enough, Lily spotted Elsie and Francis, who waved excitedly and invited Lily to join them. She pulled up a chair and gave the girls a shy smile.

"What have you been up to this summer, Lily?" Elsie asked.

"Delivering groceries for Daddy at the store," she said.

Francis smiled and asked, "How is that? It's been so hot!"

"It has been really hot, but mostly it's pretty fun. I've met some interesting people. And learned lots of interesting things about people I already knew."

"Ooooh!" Elsie squealed. "Like what?"

"Well," Lily started, lowering her voice a little, "you know Mr. Parrish, our music teacher? He has to have only very under-ripe bananas, like the greenest ones, or he gets very upset."

Elsie and Francis giggled.

"And you know Mrs. Delaney? The lady with thirteen children? They go through five pounds of bacon every two days!"

"Good thing she's got a rich husband!" Francis said, and they all laughed again.

It felt good being in the company of friendly girls and part of a little group. Before Lily left, Elsie and Francis made her promise she'd go with them to the end-of-summer picnic and that she'd sit with them at lunch when school started.

The last day at the Inlet had cheered Lily up, but her stomach tightened again when she spotted the "Mayfield – 9 miles" sign. Hazel couldn't stay away forever; Maybelle needed her help. They'd have to face each other eventually.

Monday morning came quickly. Lily had deliveries and she needed to return some books to the library, so she set out early, before Maybelle even arrived. At the library, Lily saw that she had pulled ahead of Beulah May in the contest. Then she thought of Hazel, who had read even more books than Lily or Beulah May, and she felt bad all over again.

26

HAZEL

No one said a word to Hazel about staying home from the Wagners'. Ever since the incident with Mr. Adams, they had mostly left her alone. At one point, she overheard Ma Maybelle say to Mama, "No, Estelle, it's fine. I gotta get used to being on my own without her anyway."

For a few days, Hazel stayed in her room or laid on her back under her favorite tree. When Ma Maybelle brought home *The Brownies' Book*, she read it cover to cover and then read it again. The stories helped take her mind off of Lily—until she remembered that they'd read them together.

That weekend, dark rain clouds rolled over Mayfield, in which Hazel found an exact mirror of her grief. She replayed the scene on the porch over and over in her mind, and she realized that what she felt now was anger. Had everything she and Lily shared meant nothing? Hazel didn't understand how Lily could possibly see her as the help and nothing more. And, how could she have thought that she was *helping* Hazel by what she said to Mr. Adams? Maybe she was just a spoiled white girl after all. And maybe, just maybe, it wasn't possible for colored folk and white folk to be friends. There was just too much potential for hurt.

As the rain fell, unrelenting for the next few days, her mood worsened. Not even the younger kids splashing barefoot through puddles, giggling like Christmas had come in July, could get her to smile. It physically hurt every time Hazel took a breath. She couldn't remember ever being this upset. Without Lily, it felt like a whole part of her was gone.

Hazel hadn't cried when she told Mama what Lily said. She'd seen Mama bite her lip, as if working hard to hold in her own anger, but she spoke gently and stroked Hazel's hair. She asked Hazel to tell her all the things she loved about Lily. Hazel told her about Lily's generosity, her wild impulsive ways, her newfound passion for fairness.

"I suppose, too," Hazel added, "that Lily really has only ever been around white folk and seen how they treat us and heard them talk about us. She can't know what it's like to really *be* us, even if I tell her."

"That's right. Now, could a girl like that really mean what she said?" Mama had asked. "Maybe she thought she was standing up for you. Sometimes folks have good intentions but things don't turn out like they'd like 'em to. You said yourself you know she didn't mean it. Now you gotta believe it, Hazel-girl."

Hazel sighed. "Ma Maybelle said the same thing. It just hurt so much to hear it, Mama," she said, laying her head on Mama's lap. The tears fell, hot and quick, leaving a dark stain on Mama's apron.

"I know, child. I know."

Papa's reaction was different. His face turned to stone when Mama told him what had happened. His anger was not for Lily, though.

"What that man look like, Hazel?" he demanded. Hazel gave him the best description she could, but reluctantly, scared he'd do something rash. Instead, his eyes narrowed and he said, more to himself than to the others, "Sounds just like him..." His voice trailed off.

Hazel's mind flashed to that cold November day, years ago when Papa had walked through the door with dark bruises on his arm and one eye swollen shut.

What Hazel didn't know then but knew now was that Papa was only one of four colored men in Mayfield to try to vote in the 1940 presidential election, before he'd been beaten and told that he couldn't pass the test and therefore couldn't vote. The rest of the colored folk had decided it wasn't worth a conflict with the white folk in town.

White men, with Mr. Adams leading the charge, had harassed any colored person who even registered to vote, let alone showed up on election day. But Papa, along with three men from church, had their registration cards and decided to try anyway, conflict or not. They'd agreed to not all go to City Hall at the same time, figuring they might have a better chance of not being bothered on their own.

That day, Papa had come home to a very worried Hazel and Mama with blood on his torn clothes. Mama had tenderly cleaned him up and Ma Maybelle had made him some strong coffee, but the light Hazel had seen in Papa's eyes before was gone. He didn't tell her what had happened, but even her young mind could guess.

THE DAY the rain stopped was a Sunday, and as usual, Ma Maybelle prepared a special Sunday supper for them, a low-country boil. Hazel and Willie, Jr. went to the creek, nets in hand, and caught a bucket-load of mudbugs. Ma boiled the crawfish in a special seasoning with lots of paprika and red pepper along with corn cobs, red potatoes, and a spicy sausage Mr. Wagner had given her.

That night, they ate standing around the newspaper-covered table to make room for every hungry mouth. By the time Papa and Willie, Jr. were sucking the heads of the crawfish to get every last drop of spicy goodness, Hazel was stuffed.

Mama surprised them all with a chocolate cake, complete with seven candles to celebrate Hallie's soon-to-be birthday and also the end of the summer. School would start in a few short weeks. Willie, Jr. let out a loud groan at the mention of school.

Ma Maybelle admonished him, "Oh boy, be glad for school. Your gramma never did go to school. My ma taught me to read, just barely, when we wasn't working all day in that hot sun, swatting miskeeters off us. That cotton wasn't kind to the fingers either, child. Them fingers bleed and bleed from picking out them seeds. You be grateful you get to go to school, learn all you can and remember others like me didn't get the chance."

Willie, Jr. looked down at his feet and mumbled, "Yes'm."

Hazel and Glory grinned at each other. School gave them the chance to get out of the stuffy house and not worry about working anymore. In fact, Hazel was so excited about school that she'd started reading *The Hundred Dresses* again when the dreary weather had kept her inside.

The Hundred Dresses felt different to her this time. This time, Hazel felt more tenderness toward the Maddie character. The first time she read it, Hazel had been furious that Maddie hadn't stopped Peggy from teasing Wanda. But, this time around, Hazel felt like she understood Maddie, who'd been scared that Peggy would turn on her. She'd been protecting herself; wasn't that an instinct every person had, deep down? And somehow, in understanding Maddie, she understood Lily. Lily had been frightened. Maybe she thought she was doing something gallant, yes, but also, maybe she thought he might hurt Hazel or even Lily herself if she'd said more. Maybe Lily had been protecting her.

Not the best way to go about it, she thought bitterly.

More and more, it became clear to Hazel that Lily had no way of truly understanding Hazel's life. Lily's daddy surely never got beat up for trying to cast a ballot. She didn't know what it was like to cross the street to avoid passing a white man, or how it felt to see yet another "Whites Only" sign on a building in town. She didn't know how hard it was to stand up on a rickety bus when all the seats in the back were taken, even if the front had plenty of empty ones. She didn't know what it meant to be on constant alert when she left her house, for fear of upsetting the wrong person or accidentally entering the wrong place. Speaking of wrong, Lily didn't know what it was like to feel that she was altogether wrong. Like she didn't belong any place but places where everyone looked just like her.

No, Lily didn't know what any of it was like, and she'd never have to.

It dawned on Hazel that before the day of the bridge luncheon, Lily might have never experienced the kind of hatred that Mr. Adams had shown them. Had the roles been reversed, Hazel couldn't tell herself convincingly that she'd have said anything different. And gradually, Hazel's anger faded to reveal a great sadness. Hazel knew Lily. She knew Lily felt just as bad as she did. Even so, she also knew their friendship had changed forever.

Hazel went back to help Ma Maybelle on Monday. For the

next few days, whenever she and Lily passed each other, they'd mumble a weak, "Hi," and move out of the other's way, avoiding eye contact. Since it was much too hot for anyone to leave their homes, Lily's delivery service was in high demand, so she kept herself busy and most days she came home after Hazel had already left.

On Wednesday, Lily woke to the smell of bacon and Maybelle's biscuits. As she rolled out of bed, her hand brushed Hazel's forgotten notebook underneath her mattress. She couldn't bear to look at it, and another wave of grief hit her. She still hadn't apologized to Hazel, not sure of what exactly to say or how Hazel would receive it, but she knew she should do it soon so that Hazel wouldn't think she forgot what happened on the porch.

Lily ate her breakfast and gave Maybelle a squeeze before running out the door to Daddy's store. Hazel stopped her on the porch and said, shyly, as if they'd never spoken before, "Thank you for returning *The Brownies' Book*. It really meant a lot to Miss Grace to have it in one piece." Lily didn't know what to say, so she just gave Hazel a weak smile and nodded before hurrying down the steps.

Lily's last delivery took her to the boarding house. She had looked forward to seeing Mrs. Shaw all day. After mumbling a shy greeting to Hazel's mama and Glory, she and Rose unloaded the groceries. Then Lily went to find Mrs. Shaw in the library.

When Mrs. Shaw saw her, she said, "Why, Miss Lily Wagner, look at that long face. Whatever is the matter?"

And then it all came rushing out: *The Brownies' Book*, the white girl who taught her slave to read, Mr. Adams and his foul breath, her terrible betrayal of Hazel. Mrs. Shaw listened with great patience.

"Oh, Lily. That man is an awful racist. And to take it out on children..." Mrs. Shaw reddened, anger flaring on her cheeks. Then seeing the shame written all over Lily's face, she softened a bit. "Now I know it can be hard to apolo—" but she didn't finish, because they heard the sound of breaking glass and a piercing scream coming from the front of the house. On their way to see what had happened, they heard another crash and more screams.

"Get down!" Lily heard Estelle shout. She was huddled in the hallway, her body flung across Glory's. Mrs. Shaw threw one arm protectively over Lily's chest, pinning her to the wall, and she peered into the living room. Both windows were broken and shards of glass covered the floor. For a moment, everything was quiet.

"I think they gone," Estelle said in a whisper. Mrs. Shaw crept into the room and found two large rocks. Angrily, she burst out the front door to see who had broken her windows, but came back dejected. Whoever did it was long gone. Back in the living room, she surveyed the damage.

It was then that Lily smelled the smoke. A flame rose up, enveloping one of the elegant armchairs. No one moved, stunned, until Mrs. Shaw and Estelle started shouting orders: "Go fetch a large blanket! Water! Call the fire department!" Lily and Glory hurried into the kitchen looking for a bucket to fill with water. Rose and Hetty rushed in, listened to the girls breathlessly tell what happened, and before they had even finished, Rose had dialed the fire house.

When Lily and Glory walked back to the living room, their steps slow and burdened by a heavy bucket of water, they saw Mrs. Shaw, Hetty, and Estelle using a thick curtain to smother the chair and stamp out flames on the surrounding floor. Thick black smoke filled the room and it felt like all the moisture had been sucked out of the air. Horrified, Lily saw that the sleeve of Mrs. Shaw's taffeta dress had caught fire.

"Mrs. Shaw!" she shrieked. The blaze started to move across the carpet, and Lily and Glory emptied their bucket on Mrs. Shaw and the floor, extinguishing the last of the flames. Coughing, all six of them burst onto the porch, their lungs relishing the clean air.

The fire truck pulled into the drive, and the men entered the house with their gear and tools to make sure the fire was completely out. Once they had cleared the room, they came out to speak to Mrs. Shaw. Estelle was tending to her arm, which Lily could see was red and papery-looking. Hetty, Lily noticed, had slipped out of sight, but her mind was spinning too much to wonder where she'd gone.

"Mighty brave of you to take matters into your own hands, ma'am," said a squat, sturdy fireman with the name "Jim" embroidered on his coat. "We've called Doc Macintosh. He'll be here soon."

Mrs. Shaw nodded and said impassively, "It's my home. And I had help," she added with a weak smile in the direction of the others. She couldn't hide the feverish tremor that had taken over her body.

"Lucky it wasn't worse," Jim added. "Y'all can head back in. The air's safe now that the broken window let out most of the smoke. Also, ma'am," he paused, coughing uncomfortably, "it looks like the fire was started by a flaming handkerchief tied to a rock. Smells like someone doused it in kerosene. I'm almost glad you folks were in there to stop it because it could've been a real bad fire. We've called the sheriff, he's on his way. This was no accident. We'll stay to fill him in when he arrives, but it's safe now to go on inside."

Lily couldn't move. Her feet were frozen where she stood and her heart and mind raced. *Who could have done this? And why?*

Mrs. Shaw and Estelle led the girls inside, and they peeked into the destroyed room. Lily was shocked to see how much damage the fire had caused in such a short time. The badly-burned chair resembled a skeleton, draped in a black, tattered shawl. The curtain was balled up in the corner underneath its matching partner, sagging as if saying a sweet goodbye. The beautiful teal carpet had a thick line of black soot running right through the room. The air was hazy, the floor littered with ash. It was bad, but Jim was right, it could've been a lot worse.

Estelle walked into the room and collected the two rocks that had broken the windows. One of them had a note tied to it that had been spared from the fire. She untied it and stared down at the dingy paper in her hands. Mrs. Shaw approached her slowly and with her good arm, gently took the note from her trembling fingers. It was obvious that Estelle had already read it, however, because her eyes hardened and she strode out of the room, grabbing Glory on her way out. Mrs. Shaw hung her head low, fighting back tears. Lily, unsure of what to do, walked over to Mrs. Shaw and peeked at the note. In rugged, choppy handwriting, someone had written:

Finally, you've got it right, woman. They're supposed to WORK for you, not live there. Get that filthy NEG...

Mrs. Shaw snatched it away before Lily could read the rest, but it didn't take much for her to imagine its conclusion. No wonder Estelle was angry. No wonder Mrs. Shaw's hands shook. Hetty was still nowhere to be found, but Lily was grateful that the room had been empty when the rocks had come through the windows.

Time slowed then, all around Lily. She watched silently from a corner of the room as Doc Macintosh cleaned and loosely bandaged Mrs. Shaw's arm. She listened numbly as the sheriff and his deputy questioned Mrs. Shaw about the incident. She heard Mrs. Shaw tell them that she'd received threats before. How someone had left nasty notes in the mailbox. How they'd scribbled on the side of the house and how she had to paint over it in the middle of the night. How she'd heard someone outside at strange hours, running branches along the windows, terrifying the girls. Mrs. Shaw had brushed it off as harmless vandalism, most likely done by bored teenagers.

But this. This was different. Lily heard words like "physical act of violence" and "escalating." Even though the sheriff was gruff and kept making comments under his breath that Mrs. Shaw should've expected this, his deputy, whom he called Willcox, took special care to comfort Mrs. Shaw. He put a gentle hand on her shoulder, looked at her with sad, concerned eyes, and stood protectively between her and the broken window as if he could physically shield her from pain. Lily wondered if they were friends.

As the deputy questioned Rose, Lily remembered her mischievous smirk when they'd talked about Hetty for the first time. She'd admired Rose at the time, for being unafraid, she'd thought Rose was strong and brave. But she realized now that

Rose was able to feel that way because her life wasn't in any danger. It likely never had been, until right this moment. Now, watching Rose tearfully speak to the officer, all her wild spark gone, Lily wondered if the fire would leave a permanent mark on Rose, alter her way of thinking. Because Lily saw now that Hetty couldn't afford to be that casual about Mayfield and what they would or wouldn't get angry about. For Hetty, it could mean injury. Or even death. Lily shivered at the thought.

The two policemen asked more questions of Mrs. Shaw, Estelle, and even Glory, who'd been closest to the room when the windows shattered. As they talked, Hetty rushed in with Hazel and Maybelle close behind, looking like they'd run the whole distance from Lily's house. Lily watched as they tearfully embraced Estelle and Glory, the two girls wrapped in an envelope of love; a strong grandmother and a shaken but still-standing mother. When they broke apart and everyone had been checked over for scrapes and bruises, Hazel came over to Lily and quietly sat down next to her, with Glory on her other side. Lily turned red, wet eyes toward her friend and wrapped her in a tight hug. Hazel stiffened at first, but then relaxed into Lily's arms, not letting go of her sister's hand.

That's how Daddy found Lily when he ran in and scooped her up in his strong arms. She'd never seen him so frightened. He let go to hold Lily at arm's length to make sure she was okay and gently wiped a smidge of ash off her forehead. The tears that had been silently making their way down Lily's cheeks turned into a torrential downpour.

"Oh, darlin'," Daddy said, getting down on his knees to hug her again. "It's all going to be okay now. You're safe. I'm here."

He held her tightly to his chest until her sobbing calmed. Only when she was quiet did he let her go so he could speak to the officers and Mrs. Shaw. Hazel stayed right there and sat with Lily. Daddy paused, looking down at the two girls, Hazel's smooth dark hand clutching Lily's fair, freckled one. Before he walked away, Lily saw gratitude and also a deep, deep sadness etched on his tired face.

28

HAZEL

Hazel and Glory sat next to Lily for the next several hours, Lily sitting as close as she could get to Hazel. They didn't say much as they watched the different people moving around the room. From listening to the adults, Hazel understood that someone had thrown two large rocks through the window: one to send a hateful message and the other to start what could've been a deadly fire. Mrs. Shaw's arm had been badly burned; the doctor wanted her to go to the nearest hospital, but she wouldn't. The sheriff's deputy was obviously sweet on Mrs. Shaw; he had not left her side. The other officers had spent their time checking the grass outside for any evidence (they found none), looking for escape routes (there were too many possibilities), and asking the neighbors if they'd seen anything (they hadn't).

The sheriff left, saying that he'd file reports and to let him know if anything else happened. To Hazel, it looked like they were giving up on finding the culprit, but Deputy Willcox stayed behind, his arm on Mrs. Shaw's shoulder. Hazel heard him say, "Don't worry, Maisy, love. I'm going to stay right out there in my patrol car tonight. No one's gonna hurt you or the girls under my watch."

Lily and Hazel exchanged a glance, eyebrows raised, *Maisy?* This man surely knew Mrs. Shaw on a more personal level. Mrs. Shaw relaxed and rested her head gently on Deputy Willcox's shoulder. A single tear rolled down her cheek. "Thank you, George. These girls... this home... they're my life."

But then he said, in a lower voice this time, "And maybe you oughta think about finding that girl a new place to go." At this, Mrs. Shaw picked her head up and turned away, unable to look at him.

As it turned out, once they'd all made it safely outside, Hetty had rushed out to find Ma Maybelle and Hazel, knowing that they'd want to be there. They'd been in the middle of preparing supper for the Wagners when Hetty banged on the front door of the Wagner home. The word "fire" had barely escaped her lips before all three of them ran out the door, going as fast as they could to get to Mama and Glory. They didn't know that Lily was there, too. Once back at the boarding house, Hazel heard Hetty call Wagner's Market to let Lily's father know what had happened.

They'd all been sitting at the boarding house ever since, talking in hushed tones, looking around. Mr. Wagner was the one who started the cleanup. He asked Rose and Hetty to help him find a broom and a bucket for a mop. The sudden action shook everyone from the trance of trauma and they all pitched in.

Hazel, Glory, and Lily swept up the glass shards. Hetty and Rose collected the now-ruined curtain to put outside for trash collection. Mr. Wagner dragged the burned chair and rug outside as well. Mama scrubbed the wood floor, pausing sadly when they got to the scorch mark in the middle of the room. The dark streak would not come out of the floor, and

Hazel knew that it would be an indelible stain not only on the room, but also in their memories. That the fire hadn't been worse was the only bright spot in the midst of a dark day.

Once the living room was clean, Mr. Wagner and Deputy Willcox created makeshift windows out of cardboard and plywood until new ones could be fit for the house. Mr. Wagner asked Ma Maybelle and the girls to head back to the house to prepare something for everyone to eat, nothing fancy. He said the rest of them would be there shortly.

On the short walk, Lily and Hazel fell a couple steps behind the others. Lily's shoulders still shuddered, leftover from her heaving sobs. She stared intently at the ground as she spoke.

"Hazel. About Mr. Adams. I was so wrong to say what I did. I guess I thought I was helping, but I see now that I wasn't. I've never seen you or Maybelle as 'the help' and I'm just so sorry."

"I know," Hazel said, and squeezed Lily's hand. She wouldn't say it was okay, because it wasn't. But to hear her friend acknowledge her pain was something.

"You know," Hazel went on. "I did have a good friend at school once."

"Yeah?" Lily stopped walking and turned to look at Hazel.

"Yeah. Her name was Ruby. She lived with her family just down the road from us. One night, though, her house caught fire. It was something awful. Neighbors were running with buckets and passing them down the line to put the fire out. And you know what? The Mayfield fire department never came, not even when the house was burned to ash. Thankfully, everyone made it out. But the firemen never came. And when the sheriff showed up the next day, the only thing he did was ask after Ruby's father and why he might have reason to burn his own house down. Ruby's family moved out of town, then, up North. I haven't seen her since."

Lily listened silently with wide eyes.

"You'll never get it, Lily. What it's like to be colored. I shouldn't expect you to. But I think it's good for us to learn and listen and be able to imagine what it's like for other folks. So we can take care not to hurt each other."

"You're right, Hazel. And from now on, I'm going to do just that—try to imagine what it's like for you. Before I open my big mouth."

Hazel just nodded as they reached Lily's house.

In no time at all, they had set up several options for sandwiches, fresh fruit, and a lightly dressed salad. By then, Lily's sisters and Mrs. Wagner had come home from a day trip to Columbia to shop for new school clothes. Hazel was surprised when June and even Marianne helped set the table and prepare the iced tea. They listened, wide-eyed and carefully, to the story, told first by Glory and Lily. Mama, Rose, and Hetty added more details when they arrived.

Ma Maybelle started to set the smaller table in the kitchen for her family and Hetty. Colored folk and whites never dined together, so Ma usually ate her meals in the small butler's pantry off to the side of the kitchen. But Mrs. Wagner said, "No, Maybelle. Please sit in the dining room with us."

Ma Maybelle looked at her and said, "Ma'am? You sure?"

"I'm sure."

Soon everyone gathered around the dining room table. It was a tight fit, but there was a place for everyone. Before anyone took a bite, Mr. Wagner stood up and said, "What was done today was an act of hate, and it saddens me deeply that someone in our town, our Mayfield, would stoop to this. I don't know if we'll ever know who did it, but I'm sure thankful no one was seriously hurt."

It got very quiet; everyone waited for him to say grace. Instead, he closed his eyes and began to sing in his low baritone, "When peace like a river..."

Everyone sang along, quietly at first, then with gusto, the ladies echoing him on the chorus. "It is well (it is well). With my soul (with my soul)."

After the last "soul," Mr. Wagner said, "Now, everyone's famished I'm sure, let's take advantage of this good food."

Hetty was quiet throughout the entire meal, so different from her usual bubbly demeanor. But right before they had dessert, she mumbled something, so quiet that Lily's mother, who had been talking about how to approach the townspeople about the fire, barely heard her. "Hetty? Did you say something, dear?"

Everyone turned to look at the beautiful young woman sitting so close to the corner of the room it seemed like she hoped the walls would swallow her up. Louder this time, Hetty said, "This all happened because of me."

Estelle stood, pushing her chair out from the table, scraping the floor loudly. Crouching so that she could meet Hetty's eye, Estelle put her hands on either side of the girl's face and lifted her head slightly so Hetty would look at her. "Now, you listen to me, child. This ain't your fault. This happened because someone's heart's so hardened by hate they can't see what we see: a strong, smart, beautiful young lady."

"Even so, I think it's best if I go on ho..." Hetty started to say, but she wasn't able to finish.

"Absolutely not!" Mrs. Shaw said firmly. "You are to finish the summer with me. You're not to leave until you've found a teaching job like we planned." Her voice softened as she added, "Of course, that is, if you *want* to stay. I'd really like it if you did."

Hetty looked frightened, but Mrs. Shaw continued. "And

George, er, Deputy Willcox will keep us safe."

Hetty nodded and wiped a tear as Ma's voice broke through the silence. "Time for something sweet! Lucky Hazel finished hand-cranking that peach custard this morning."

The cool, summery treat gave everyone a chance to forget about the day's horrors.

HAZEL, Glory, Mama, and Ma Maybelle stayed at the Wagners' long after Mrs. Shaw, Hetty, and Rose walked back to the boarding house. Mrs. Shaw was still shaken, but she had to write the other girls, who thankfully had been vacationing with their families.

Lily's family helped Hazel's clean up after the impromptu dinner party. June pitched in to dry the dishes. They did everything in a solemn silence, and in the end, the Wagners' kitchen sparkled so that it looked like it had never been used.

Since it was late, Mr. Wagner offered to drive the Jacksons home, and they gratefully accepted. Hazel knew Ma's joints were aching and Mama was tired. It had been a very long day. Lily gave Hazel a quick squeeze before they headed out the door and whispered a simple, "Thank you for staying by me today."

In some ways, Hazel felt like things with Lily were exactly the way they'd been before Mr. Adams, but in other ways, she knew that everything had changed. Despite that, Hazel was sure of one thing: that she'd worried just as much about Lily as she did about her sister and her mother, a feeling she'd never felt for a single person outside her family. And she realized in that moment that it didn't matter what color skin they had. What mattered was that the two girls had become true, bosom friends, as their dear Anne with an "E" would say.

During the car ride home, Ma Maybelle sat up front with Mr. Wagner, the other three comfortably close in the back, but no one said a word. Glory leaned her head against Mama's arm and closed her eyes. Hazel looked out the window, saying a quick prayer over the boarding house as they passed it. *Dear Lord, please keep them safe. Please keep our friends safe.* Hazel doubted very much that anyone there could sleep. She could've sworn the car slowed down ever so slightly as they drove by, and she wondered if Lily's daddy was praying a prayer of his own.

When the car finally pulled up to Hazel's house, Mr. Wagner cleared his throat and spoke in a tired, gravelly voice. "Maybelle, thank you for dinner and for taking care of everybody tonight."

Ma looked at him kindly and said, "It's nothing, Mr. Wagner, don't you think on it."

He continued, "Estelle and Glory, I'm so sorry for what happened today, but, and I mean this from the bottom of my heart, I'm so thankful you're both okay. I hope you'll consider still working for Mrs. Shaw. She's a fine woman."

Mama sniffed, hiding her face, but said shakily, "Oh yes sir. Mrs. Shaw done showed us we matter to her today. We'll go on back tomorrow and help her clean up the rest."

Lily's daddy nodded. He turned around to face Hazel, who sat directly behind him. "And Hazel," his voice cracked, "There's no way I could thank you enough for taking care of my girl today. She's real special, my Lily Jo. And so are you."

Hazel whispered, "Lily's the best friend I ever had, sir."

And he looked her right in the eye and said, "She's mighty lucky to have you."

They climbed out of the car, wished Mr. Wagner a good night, and stood in a little group on the front step, watching his car get smaller and smaller as he drove away. Ma Maybelle said,

"Lawd, what a day. Ima go straight to bed." Mama wrapped her girls in a tight hug and kissed the tops of their heads. They didn't speak as they entered the house, careful not to wake the younger children. Hazel saw Mama slip Miss Essie a shiny quarter and heard her whisper, "Thank you so much for staying."

Miss Essie whispered back, "I'm mighty glad y'all all right." After tiptoeing into Mama's room, Hazel and Glory fell soundly asleep.

THE NEXT MORNING, before any of them could leave the house, they found neighbors crowded around the door, waiting to hear all about the fire. *News sure travels fast around here,* Hazel thought. They gave their friends just enough to satisfy their curiosity, and the four of them headed to the bus stop.

Hazel felt different that morning, like she'd come to a major point in her short life. One that would be a defining line between the before-the-fire Hazel and the after-the-fire Hazel. As they walked, Hazel looped her arm in her sister's and they fell a step behind the older women. It seemed obvious to the whole world, or maybe just to Hazel, that the four of them were an unstoppable force, a team to be reckoned with. With pride welling in her chest, Hazel watched Mama and Ma Maybelle walk back toward the white side of town, chins up, heads held high. They weren't trying to be unseen or remain nameless colored women. They would not let hate win. In the kitchen that morning, Mama had told Hazel and Glory very seriously, "Girls, we gonna be brave. We not gonna let them white folk think we scared. We gonna go on and do our jobs like we supposed to."

"Yes'm," they'd answered together.

They got off the bus and walked to the boarding house. A lump caught in Hazel's throat as she watched Mama and Glory walk up the front steps. She noticed two things right away. The first was that Deputy Willcox had parked a sheriff's department car right outside Mrs. Shaw's, and it looked like he'd been there all night, his face unshaven, his hair unruly. The second thing was that someone—Hazel guessed Rose—had filled a planter on the porch with bright wildflowers.

"Hey Glory! Bring Deputy Willcox some coffee and a biscuit, will you?" Hazel said to her sister. Glory grinned and waved goodbye to Hazel, who took Ma Maybelle's hand and kept walking.

"How you holdin' up, Sugar?"

"I think I'm okay. It's just, I know that hateful things happen. Miss Grace taught us a lot, and I've seen a lot myself. But it's hard not to feel scared all the time, even though I don't want to."

"I know, child. It's hard to understand why the world is the way it is. And even in such a small town like Mayfield. But keep your chin up. I got a feeling things'll get better one day."

Hazel couldn't help but feel cheered by her optimism.

When they arrived at the Wagners', they were bombarded by a sweet aroma. Surprised, they found Lily, June, and Mrs. Wagner in the kitchen, making a huge mess but besides that, cooking pancakes and frying bacon.

"It won't be quite as good as yours, Maybelle," Mrs. Wagner said when she saw them come in. "But we wanted to say thank you for everything you did yesterday. Come on in, sit. Fresh orange juice?"

Ma Maybelle hesitated, for just a second. Before last night, she'd not been invited to share their table. But Mrs. Wagner noticed the worry on her face.

"It's all right, Maybelle," Mrs. Wagner started. "Over the

last few weeks, I've learned a couple of things. First is that you are part of this family, you always have been. Second is that I've been doing things the way everyone else does, in ways that keep us separate from each other rather than together. I know now that's just not right." Then, she smiled wide and said brightly, "Come on, breakfast is our treat today!"

June poured glasses of juice and set the table with her mother's best china and the silver, and Lily finished cooking. Marianne, as usual, was nowhere to be found. Soon, each plate had a small stack of steaming fluffy pancakes and a thick, crispy piece of bacon. Lily's mother said grace, and they ate breakfast together. Lily had made Hazel's pancakes special, sprinkling in a few chocolate chips, and Hazel grinned as she doused them in syrup.

"What a nice surprise, Missus Wagner," Ma Maybelle said in between bites. "Sure tastes good."

"Well, I'd expect so, Maybelle, since Lily's learned to cook from watching you," Mrs. Wagner replied, a kind smile lighting her face.

As they ate, they asked about Mama and Glory and wondered how the ladies at the boarding house were faring. Mrs. Wagner told them she'd called over there and found out from Rose that Mrs. Shaw was in a lot of pain but that the burn looked to be healing.

When breakfast was over, everyone pitched in to clean up before they went their separate ways. Lily stuck around, though, to share the morning with Hazel. Ma Maybelle, spared from the breakfast preparation and cleanup, told them to go on and run around for a bit. She wouldn't need any help for a while.

The girls went right upstairs to start a new book together.

29

LILY

The next day was the end-of-summer school picnic, at which they'd announce the winners of the reading contest. Lily had no idea where she'd ended up in the contest because the incident with Mr. Adams and then the fire had changed everything. She had checked in with Miss Nora the day before but didn't see the ledger. *Oh well*, she thought. Over the course of just a few days, she'd learned that some things were more important than winning a contest.

It was a beautiful day for a picnic: sunny, clear skies peppered with scattered wispy clouds, the slightest hint of a breeze offering relief from the heat. As she walked alone to meet her classmates, she thought more about the terrible, awful thing that had happened with Mr. Adams. Even though she'd apologized, Lily still felt horrible. The kind of horrible that kept her awake at night. The kind of horrible that shrouded her mind in a dark cloud, threatening to consume her for the rest of her days.

Lily had come to understand why she'd said what she did. She'd thought she was helping, that Hazel needed a defender.

But Hazel didn't need saving. Hazel was the one who saved Lily from the snake bite and Tremaine from his breathing episode. Hazel was her own kind of force in this world, and all she needed was a friend who regarded her as her own, brave person.

Lily knew, too, that it was easy to talk of injustice and inequality and the evil that was racism, but when actually faced with a conflict, Lily had failed herself.

And she'd failed Hazel.

She felt just as responsible as the hateful person who'd thrown the rocks at the boarding house. Worse, even, because she'd betrayed a friend, someone she cared for. Lily had made Hazel feel like less than she was, and she didn't know how she'd ever make up for that. Yet still, in Hazel's strong and quiet way, she had forgiven Lily and, Lily supposed, she'd have to forgive herself.

Elsie and Francis shouted a cheerful, "Hey, Lily!" interrupting her thoughts, as they approached the corner. Lily smiled, grateful to have company for the rest of the walk.

"What was it like, the fire?" Francis asked.

"It was so scary. I'm glad nobody got hurt," was all Lily could say.

"Me, too," Elsie said. "My uncle Jim is the firefighter who came right after. He said the damage wasn't too bad because you ladies helped put out the fire. You're so brave, Lily! I'd have positively frozen with fright and burned up!"

Lily laughed, "No you wouldn't. You'd have done the same thing. I wasn't even thinking, just did what I had to. But tell your Uncle Jim thanks for me, okay? He was real nice after the fire."

Elsie nodded and looped her arm in Lily's, Francis did the same on Elsie's left, and the trio walked along to the picnic.

Lily couldn't believe the summer was almost over; it had

certainly been eventful. If someone had told her the day the reading contest was announced that she would have read some inspiring and important books, she might've believed them. But, if someone had told her she'd become close friends with Maybelle's granddaughter, look up to someone she'd feared, survive a rattlesnake bite, betray her best friend in the world, and help put out a fire, she'd have looked at that someone like she'd grown two heads.

Lily was content and peaceful as she walked toward the library, but anxious to hear the results of the contest. "How many books did you read, girls?"

Elsie and Francis giggled sheepishly, and Elsie mumbled, "I ran out of time" at the same time Francis said, "I got too busy."

"I'm sure that ol' Beulah May Porter will win anyway," Francis continued. "That girl reads all the time. It's a wonder she has time to do anything else."

Lily was taken aback by Francis's words. Could there be such a thing as reading too much? She decided right there that, yes, she supposed that reading too much might mean that a person could miss out on her own life happening right around her. But Lily also knew that not reading at all would rob a person of finding magic and wonder and meeting new friends completely unlike themselves and traveling to places completely unlike home.

It's all a balancing act, then, Lily thought. If she'd spent all summer reading, she'd have missed out on Hazel, missed getting to know Hetty and Rose and Mrs. Shaw, missed the fishing adventure with Daddy at the Inlet, and missed listening to Aunt Margaret's stories. Sometimes it was important to put the book down.

But oh, she was glad to have met Anne and Mary and Wanda. She'd not soon forget them or the lessons they'd taught her: that friendship and kindness are two of the greatest joys in life, and that you can't have one without the other. They'd also taught her, perhaps more importantly, that first impressions aren't everything. True friendships happen over time, when people slowly open themselves up to one another, to truly be seen, for all their good and all their flaws.

Last night, it had occurred to Lily that as summer came to an end, she wouldn't see Hazel much anymore. Maybelle wouldn't bring her to the house because she'd be in her own school, hopefully making new friends of her own. The thought had, at first, deeply saddened Lily. But she had a feeling that her friendship with Hazel went much deeper than all that. It would take more than separate schools to dissolve a friendship like theirs. Now, she smiled as an idea about how they could stay in touch formed in her mind, but it would have to wait. The girls had arrived at the picnic right on time.

"Gather round! Gather round!" Mr. Edwards shouted in a jolly voice. He stood on the steps of the Mayfield Public Library and projected his voice rather impressively across the lawn. The students were gathered on the grass, under the crepe myrtles, their pink petals starting to fall, signaling to the world that they'd had just about enough of the heat. The shade didn't provide much relief, but at least it got them out of the sun. Mr. Edwards' voice brought everyone closer to the steps, ready to hear what he had to say.

"Welcome students! I trust that everyone had a great summer, but boy, it's been a hot one!" As if he'd rehearsed it, he paused to wipe the sweat from his pink forehead. "Let's begin our beautiful picnic day with the best part, the food! We owe a great thanks to Wagner's Market for the sandwiches and fruit, and to Jean's for the popsicles. What a treat for us all!"

The teachers spread colorful patchwork quilts on the grass and placed a basket of food on each one. Lily found a blanket in the shade to share with Elsie and Francis and a couple of the other girls from their class. As they ate—popsicles first, so they wouldn't melt!—they talked about the summer. Almost every one of them had spent time at the Inlet, living up to its nickname of "Little Mayfield." They chatted with nervous excitement about starting junior high, how they'd change classes and have different teachers, some of whom they'd met already at the picnic. And oh, the homework was rumored to be awful! But Lily never minded schoolwork. She just hoped they'd assign her some decent books to read.

When the food was gone, Mr. Edwards walked up front, this time accompanied by Miss Nora. Conversations stopped and the students looked up at him in anticipation.

"Miss Nora tells me you all read quite a lot this summer, which is exactly what we'd hoped for! She told me she's been impressed with your level of maturity and responsibility, which are virtues we hope you'll carry into next school year."

The teachers clapped, and Mr. Edwards continued. "Now, I know you're eager to hear the results of our contest. Before we do that, though, let's have a round of applause for everyone who read even one book this summer. You are one book smarter than you were in June, and that's worth celebrating!" A louder round of applause broke out, and a group of rowdy boys let out shrill whistles.

"Okay, okay, settle down," Mr. Edwards said with a grin. "Let's begin with the awards." He paused for dramatic effect.

"Third prize goes to Beaumont Adams!" At the sound of her old friend's name, Lily looked up. She couldn't believe he read so much and was grateful Elsie and Francis hadn't asked her about him. Beau turned red and reluctantly got up from his seat on the lawn, ignoring the taunting comments from his friends.

"Congratulations, son," Mr. Edwards said. "As promised, there is a prize, but you must choose what it is you'd like: a shiny new fifty-cent piece or a brand-new book from Miss Pearl's. It's your choice."

Beau, embarrassed, mumbled his answer and Mr. Edwards handed him a shiny coin and clapped him on the back. Then Beau went back to his seat, sneaking a glance at Lily, who kept her eyes resolutely on Mr. Edwards.

"Second prize goes to... Beulah May Porter!" Everyone turned to look at Beulah May, who wore a forced smile, but actually looked like she might cry. Lily's heart soared. Had she really managed to win?

Beulah May hardly took even a second to decide about her prize. Smiling sweetly up at Mr. Edwards, she said "I'll take a book, please," which earned her a collective groan from the crowd. Lily rolled her eyes. *We are sitting on the lawn of a building full of free books. Why'd she give up fifty cents for that?*

Mr. Edwards handed Beulah May a neatly-wrapped book, and she flounced down the steps with her nose in the air like she couldn't be bothered by the lowly peasants on the lawn.

"And finally... first prize goes to... Lillian Wagner! She read a whopping thirty books this summer!"

The girls around Lily squealed and looked at her, impressed. Lily's heart raced as she climbed the steps.

"Congratulations, Miss Wagner," Mr. Edwards boomed. "What'll it be? A new book or a crisp new dollar bill?"

"I'll take the money!" she said, a little too quickly, and heard a laugh from the crowd. "Only because, you know, our beautiful library gives us books for free."

Miss Nora beamed, and Beulah May scowled at her, but Lily didn't care. She knew exactly how she would use her money. Lily felt the next words coming up out of her mouth before she could stop them.

"But," she said loudly, "there's someone who read more books than I did. Her name's Hazel Jackson, and she wasn't allowed in the contest because she goes to the colored school. She's the one who really deserves first place. She read thirty-eight and I know because—"

Mr. Edwards' smile disappeared, and he cleared his throat nervously, interrupting her. "That's quite enough Miss Wagner, thank you. Here's your prize."

Looking like he'd rather be anywhere else in the world, Mr. Edwards ushered Lily off the stage and started in on another incredibly corny speech about growing up and new beginnings and all of that, but Lily barely listened.

The girls on Lily's blanket stared at her as she made her way back to them. Elsie was the first to speak. "Congratulations, Lily! I didn't know you liked to read that much!"

"Neither did I, really. It was Hazel who reminded me how fun it is."

Dorothy Hammonds, who'd joined them for lunch, had a disgusted look on her face, much like the one Beau had the night of the parade. "So, it's true then, huh? Just like your father. I didn't believe it when my brother told me, but now I do. C'mon Betty," she said, grabbing her best friend's wrist, "let's go. This dumb picnic's over anyway."

Elsie and Francis watched them go but stayed firmly seated where they were. "How do you know that girl—Hazel, is it?— read all those books?" Francis asked.

"Because we read some of them together," Lily said calmly, as if the exchange with Dorothy hadn't even happened.

"What's it like to be friends with a colored girl?" Elsie seemed curious rather than hateful, so Lily shrugged.

"Not much different than being friends with anyone else. Hazel's really smart and a good friend. She even saved my life this summer. She's just like us, she just goes to a different school, that's all."

Elsie and Francis nodded and smiled, but Lily could tell the smiles were forced.

"Is there a problem?" she asked them, her face heating up.

Elsie pursed her lips and Frances turned red. "No, no, it's just that, you know, we could never do it. Our parents, they'd be so mad."

Lily understood this; she'd watched how Mr. Adams treated Beau for years and how finally his hatred had seeped into his son, who was more afraid of his father than anything else. So, Lily understood what Elsie said, even though she knew now that parents were capable of being very wrong.

"What Francis means is, you know, our parents aren't like yours," Elsie said, stumbling through her words. Lily could tell they both didn't want to make this a big deal or let it get in the way of them being friends.

"I think they just stopped worrying so much about what other people thought. It's a lesson we all could learn," she said, her voice firm but kind.

Elsie and Francis relaxed a bit, nodded, then started walking toward home.

"Well," Francis said, changing the subject. "Thirty books! The look on Beulah May's face was hysterical. You'll give her a run for her money in junior high." Lily smiled and listened to Elsie and Francis carry on about seventh grade and giggle about the boys, but her mind was on Hazel and what she'd tell her when she got home.

At the corner where they would go their separate ways, Lily said, "I need to get home to tell everyone the news. See you at school?"

Elsie grinned and said, "Seventh grade is going to be so much fun, Lily! Don't forget to sit with us at lunch the first day! Never you mind what Dorothy Hammonds thinks."

30

HAZEL

Hazel was in the kitchen helping Ma Maybelle when Lily burst through the front door and into the kitchen. Feigning embarrassment, she collected herself, smoothed down her skirt, got a glass of water, and sat down at the table. Hazel stared at her, but Ma Maybelle spoke first. "Well, child? You win that contest or not?"

Lily grinned. "Yes! I couldn't believe it! Now Maybelle, I'm gonna need to borrow Hazel for a while, 'kay?"

"Wait, wait, wait, hold on. You beat Beulah May?" Hazel asked.

"Yup! Now, c'mon Hazel!" Lily grabbed her hand and pulled her out the door before Ma could say another word.

Hazel struggled to keep up and managed to yell, "Where... are... we... going?" between breaths.

Lily slowed then, dropped Hazel's hand, and stopped. "Sorry! I'm just so excited."

"But, Lily. We shouldn't be seen together out and about. You know that."

"I know I haven't been very good about putting myself in

your shoes, Hazel. With how Beau and Mr. Adams acted, I know that us being together is dangerous. But it's wrong that we can't be friends, and I want you to know I believe that with all my heart. My daddy was brave to open the doors of his store, and we're going to be brave today, too. I'm not taking you anywhere you don't have a right to be, and we can walk a little farther apart on the street. If at any point you wanna come home, you just tell me and we will, no question."

"Okay," Hazel said, after considering it for a minute. "You're right. Let's go."

Lily pulled out the dollar bill and handed it to Hazel.

"What's that for?" she asked.

"Prize money. I have a surprise!"

Lily started walking again, but this time at a more manageable pace. Hazel shoved the dollar bill in the pocket of her dress as she tried to keep up. She couldn't believe Lily would just hand over money like that, but she didn't have time to think about it. They headed toward Main Street, Lily on a mission and Hazel wondering what her crazy friend was up to.

This was one of the last days they'd have to spend together, and Hazel glanced at Lily in a different light, as if she wanted to hold this memory of Lily in her mind, exactly as she was right then: frizzy red curls, freckles peering through flushed cheeks, a wild look in her eyes like she was ready for anything, arms swinging determinedly by her sides, feet placed purposefully with each step, not a hint of hesitation. Hazel loved Lily's passionate and spontaneous nature as well as her adventurous spirit, and she wondered if all redheads shared similar personality traits, much like their beloved Anne of Green Gables.

It was hot, and Hazel was grateful when Lily stopped walking. They had passed all the busy shops on Main Street, and ended up at Pearl's, the very last shop, set apart from the others, as close to the colored side of town as a Main Street business could get. Pearl's was empty of customers, dark inside but clearly open.

Lily grabbed her hand and led her inside.

Hazel had only been in Pearl's once before, a long time ago, with Papa. But it felt like time had stood still since then. Stacks of books in every size, color, and subject lined the walls. A collection of children's books sat up front with beautiful illustrations and hand-painted covers.

She remembered Papa telling her that Pearl's had been vandalized, years ago—broken windows, ugly words and symbols painted on the walls. A rumor circulated that she wasn't actually white, that she only appeared white but had some colored blood in her. But Pearl was known to be a stubborn old bat—she never gave an answer to the rumor, just cleaned up and resumed business as usual. Since she was the only bookseller for miles around, white folk ended up forgetting the rumors and still came in for books. However, Pearl's was the only shop in all of Mayfield that had never used a back door or put up any "Whites Only" signs.

The girls inhaled sharply, breathing in all the dust and old-book smell, then turned to each other and giggled. Is this how normal people reacted in a bookstore? An older woman with silver hair tied in a loose bun and spectacles on the tip of her nose stood on a ladder in the back, shelving books.

"Welcome girls! How can I help you today?" she asked. If Miss Pearl thought anything of a white girl and a colored girl standing in her store holding hands, she didn't let on.

Lily spoke up. "Miss Pearl, we'd like to buy two books, please. The thing is, we don't have very much money. You have a resale selection, right?"

The old woman smiled. "Yes! And I've just added more to it today. Come look!" She led them to a tall shelf toward the middle of the store. The books on this shelf were well-loved;

yellowed pages, scuffed covers, some held together by spines so tattered that the girls couldn't make out the titles. Lily turned to Hazel and said, "The books on this shelf cost five cents each. Pick anything you like. Better if you can find two copies of something so we can read it together!"

Hazel replied, "Or, we get two good ones and then trade when we're through?"

Lily grinned and said, "Even better."

They picked their way through the books, Lily starting at the top on her tippy toes, Hazel at the bottom, sitting cross-legged on the floor.

In the end, Lily chose a classic story about a pioneer family finding their way and building their life in the brand-new frontier. Hazel chose a juicy-looking murder mystery featuring a detective named Poirot. They paid Miss Pearl and, clutching their purchases to their chests, headed back outside, squinting their eyes in the bright sunshine.

At the very end of Main Street, they stopped at a large oak tree, standing guard like a sign that they had left downtown. Hazel knew that most white folks didn't walk much further than this. Beyond the tree was the colored part of town, and the large tree had always felt like a marker to Hazel, a signal that one side was one thing but the other side was a whole different thing. To Hazel, the colored side was home. It was warm and safe and the place where she could relax and just be. The white side was where she always had to worry about her words, what her face was doing, where she walked. She wondered, for a brief minute, if Lily's feelings were the same, just in reverse.

Breaking her train of thought, Lily said, "Hazel! Look at that knothole!"

Indeed, there was a deep hole about halfway up the tree, one that neither girl could reach without climbing. It was dark and mysterious and inviting. They scampered up the branches until they reached the knothole and sat on opposite sides of it.

"I've been thinking," Lily started cautiously, "if you want..."

"Yeah?" Hazel asked.

"Let's keep up our notebook when school starts. We'll be like pen pals, but not mess with stamps and the post office. We can use this knothole to keep the journal and even pass books back and forth to each other! It's deep enough no one would see."

"What if it rains?" Hazel asked.

"We'll keep it in an old cigar box. I have one at home. That way, it will be safe from water and animals."

"Okay," said Hazel. "How will we know when to check it?"

"How about on Saturdays? That way we each have a week with it. We'll only use the knothole if we happen to miss each other, coming or going."

"I like that idea!" said Hazel. "It'll be our secret." She paused to give Lily a meaningful look. "I'm sure going to miss spending the days with you."

Lily climbed over so she was sitting on Hazel's sturdy branch and laid her head on Hazel's shoulder. "I know, me too. But at least this way, we don't have to stop being friends."

They sat for a few more minutes, soaking in the warm sunlight and the last of the summer. "Now, can you stay here for a few minutes?" Lily said. "We still have money and I have one more surprise!"

Hazel nodded and watched her friend clamber down from the tree and take off running. She liked sitting up in that tree, and she had a good book to read, too.

Just as Hazel was finding out who got murdered and what Poirot's plan was to follow clues, Lily came back. Her hands were full and she hollered, "Come on down! Let's sit in the shade!"

Hazel carefully climbed down and plopped herself on the soft grass. Lily held out a glass full to the brim with Jean's famous chocolate shake, thick and creamy, topped with whipped cream, only a little melted from her walk over. Lily had one just like it, and Hazel took her own slowly, unsure.

"Jean just let you walk outta there with a couple of her glasses?" Hazel asked, ignoring how her mouth was watering for a taste of the cool, creamy chocolate.

"She doesn't have to know," Lily giggled. "Besides, I'll take them back. It was crowded and lots of folks were taking food and drinks outside."

Shaking her head again at Lily's boldness and certainty, Hazel sighed and took a long, sweet sip from her straw. The girls leaned back against the tree, slurping their shakes and breathing in the heat of the afternoon, one of the last of the summer. After the glasses were empty, and the whipped cream properly licked clean off the sides, Lily pressed the coins that were left from the dollar into Hazel's hand and said, "Keep it. It's really yours anyway. You read more books than I did. In my mind, you're the true winner of that contest."

Hazel grinned. She knew then, beyond any doubt, that for all her other grand misunderstandings of the summer, Lily had learned one important thing. She could have dragged her to Jean's with her. The Lily Hazel met in June would have done just that. But Jean's was not a place where Hazel would be welcomed. Lily knew the importance of keeping Hazel safe in this world and she loved her like a real friend, not just "the help."

"You know," Lily went on, "I've been thinking about this summer. And all the things that happened. I think you need to write a story about it."

"Me?" Hazel said, surprised.

"Yes, you. We need stories about brave colored girls just like you, Hazel."

Hazel liked the idea of this. She thought of Glory and Hallie and Tremaine and little Nell, who deserved to read stories about children that looked like them. But Hazel wasn't sure she could do it.

"I'm not all that brave, Lily."

Lily's mouth dropped in surprise. "How could you think that? You saved my life, Hazel. I wouldn't be standing here if you didn't know what to do with that snake bite. You saved Tremaine's life. You stood your ground with Doc Macintosh and didn't let Beau or Mr. Adams get the best of you. There's gotta be a story in all of that, don't you think? One with you as the hero, as the Anne or the Mary Lennox. Just think of it, Hazel Jackson, girl wonder." Lily leaned back against the tree.

When Hazel saw herself through Lily's eyes, everything changed. She'd thought, throughout all of the things Lily had just described, that she hadn't done anything miraculous. That she was just moving through her life. But Lily was right. She had done all those things. And, at that moment, she felt like anything in the world was possible.

The two girls sat together under the leaves of the oak tree until dusk and simply enjoyed one another. All the fear and uncertainty had left Hazel, and just like in Ma Maybelle's favorite hymn, it was, truly, well with her soul.

31

SEPTEMBER 1945

Dear Lily,

I hope you find this right where I left it and that a pack (flock?) of owls don't run off with it first. Ma Maybelle tells me that you started school the same day I did. I hope your first day was as good as mine. We got a wonderful surprise! Miss Grace moved up to teach junior high! I was so happy when I walked in the classroom, I thought I'd burst. We are learning so much.

The other surprise is that Glory has a new teacher, too... a young, pretty, brand-new teacher... have you guessed yet? It's Hetty! Glory told me she's staying with Miss Grace. Miss Harriet, her official teacher name, told her class she's so happy to live in the neighborhood where her students live. I just know she's going to be a great teacher.

Tremaine's doing well, thanks for asking. Willie Jr. is a mess as always, getting in trouble at school and Mama says he'll give her gray hairs before her time. Hallie started second grade and she asks us so many questions at dinner it's a wonder her head doesn't spin clean off. And baby Nell is still the sweetest, but she started talking. We hope she doesn't learn from Hallie how to talk and talk and talk or we'll never have any peace around here.

I met a new girl named Lavender. She's brand new to Mayfield, and we're going to start a literary journal for our school. We both like to write, and we found a small group of other students who do too. Every month, we'll ask people to submit poems and short stories, and then we'll publish it to hand out to the rest of the class. Miss Grace is going to help. I can't wait to give you a copy of our first issue!

Well, I suppose it's time to go stick this in our secret hiding spot. Before I go though, I want to tell you about a poem we're reading in school that I thought you'd like. It's called "I, Too" by Langston Hughes. He talks about how in his perfect world, we'd all be around the same table, colored folks and white folks alike. Nobody would get left in the kitchen, but we'd all be together. It reminded me of the night of the fire. How we all gathered at your house afterward, and we all ate together, and no one mentioned the rules, or propriety, or separation. We were just one family of human beings. It's a night I'll never forget. I think moments like that work to get us all a little closer to Mr. Hughes' idea of the American Dream.

All my love,
Hazel Clementine

Dearest Hazel,

I'm so glad you are enjoying school and that Miss Grace is teaching you again! I'm sure Hetty is doing a great job, too.

Marianne has a "beau" already, which is mostly driving Daddy crazy. She's making June and me wait for hours to get in the bathroom in the morning since she insists on spending forever getting the waves in her hair just right.

Elsie and Francis have turned out to be nice girls and there's now a group of us that sit together at lunch. Even Beulah May's joined us. I think she was lonely, but instead of just staying quiet, she acted like she was better than everyone, a habit she's still trying to break. She's all right, I guess.

Having friends makes school less lonely for me, but my heart aches for our chats and summer afternoons together. I do wish we could go to the same school. I feel like when we talk, it's about more important things than just the usual junior high gossip and boy talk. Plus, no one loves to read as much as we do.

Thanks for telling me about the Langston Hughes poem. It felt like Providence since the exact day I read your letter, we read a poem in class too. It was written by a Mr. Robert Frost. Here are the last lines for you:

"I shall be telling this with a sigh,
somewhere ages and ages hence:
two roads diverged in a wood,
and I—I took the one less traveled by,
and that has made all the difference."

Miss Bradley, our language teacher, asked us to think of a time we did something that wasn't the way most folks did things. I thought of the day you and I met. I suppose I had a choice then, to only see how different we were and shy away, or to see you as a friend. I'm so glad I chose the latter. But, I'm also glad you took the second path, too. I don't imagine that many smart girls like you would've given a wild and silly white girl a chance. So, thank you, Hazel. I do believe it has made "all the difference," as Mr. Frost writes. I can't wait to hear from you again.

Love, Lily

AUGUST 28, 1963

It was 8:58 AM, two minutes until they were supposed to meet. Hazel smoothed her brown tweed skirt and jacket, an outfit she'd purchased mostly for her teaching interviews years back. Since then, she'd been teaching high school English in Harlem, New York.

Like Miss Grace before her, Hazel knew how to spark interest in her students and give them hope for the future. Her classroom was a safe haven, a place where her students could laugh and cry and enjoy stories, and most of all, tell their own. Inspired by *The Brownies' Book* of her childhood, Hazel's class published an anthology every year titled, *Heroes of Harlem*, in which every student added a favorite poem or short story they'd written. The anthologies were Hazel's most prized possessions, and she kept them on a special shelf in her classroom, "all lined up," just like Wanda's hundred dresses. Every time a student felt discouraged or angry or just tired of life, she sent them to the *Heroes of Harlem*, to the ones who had come before.

In the evenings, Hazel went home to write. Because she'd had no books to read about girls like herself when she was a child, she wrote books for young people about a girl named Clementine, a curious, sassy, and smart colored girl in small-town South Carolina.

Hazel glanced at her watch, 9:05, and sighed. *Typical Lily*, she thought.

Her mind flashed back to the summer after her senior year of high school. Ma Maybelle had grown ill and could not work. Hazel spent the summer working for the Wagners until they could find someone else. There came a day when Hazel walked in and Ma Maybelle struggled to sit up. And when Ma's labored breathing eventually slowed and she lay still, Lily had been at Hazel's side, almost the next instant. She hadn't left until the funeral was over and all the casseroles had been eaten. Now, the memory filled Hazel's eyes with tears, and she quickly wiped them away.

Where is she? Hazel wondered, impatient to see her old friend.

When Hazel left to attend a two-year women's teaching college in Charleston, Lily had gone to Winthrop College, also to become a teacher. When she graduated, however, she was admitted to Clemson as one of the university's first female students and studied journalism. Now, she wrote for *The Washington Post*, covering civil rights issues, like the bus boycott in Montgomery and Dr. King's peaceful marches. When Hazel asked Lily to meet her here today, she had agreed right away.

They'd stayed in touch throughout the years—writing back and forth using their secret knothole in the tree until the journal was tattered and torn, evidence of a beautiful friend-ship between two brave girls, flowing against the grain of what society had dictated for them. They spent as much of the summers as they could together, sharing favorite books with each other. During college and the years that followed, they'd continued to write.

Even so, Hazel hadn't seen her friend in a few years. Her heart sped up in anticipation, and a bead of sweat made its way down her face in the blazing mid-morning sun.

Hazel gazed across the reflecting pool toward the Lincoln Memorial, where she could see a crowd already forming. She felt a hand on her arm and heard an excited squeal behind her. When she turned around, she was wrapped up in a familiar embrace, topped off by a head of unruly red curls. Hazel squeezed Lily and pulled back to look at her properly. Lily wore a pretty blue floral dress and she had grown up, but her light freckled skin and shining smile had not changed one bit.

"Ready, Hazel?" Lily asked.

"Ready!" she replied. Lily grabbed her hand, just as they'd done as girls. They walked across the mall and reached the crowd just in time to hear Dr. King's voice ring out, loud and clear.

As they settled in to listen to Dr. King talk about dreams and equality and justice, Hazel looked at Lily and smiled at the memories that flooded her mind. They had certainly made a lot of grand ones over the years. But standing there, hand in hand, with silent tears streaming down their faces, Hazel knew that neither one of them would ever forget that first summer, the one where they learned lasting truths about their hometown, the world, each other, and most of all, themselves.

AUTHOR'S NOTE

This story is a work of historical fiction, including the characters and the town of Mayfield. But Lily's character, red curls and all, was inspired by my grandmother, Norma Willcox Bradley Thornbrough. My grandmother was the third of four Willcox girls, and their father did, indeed, own a grocery store. Much like Mr. Wagner, my great-granddaddy Willcox was a kind man, and generous, too.

Even though this story takes place after World War II, my grandmother spent her early childhood in small-town South Carolina during the Great Depression. She remembers not having a lot of money and how her town was segregated.

Just like Lily, Grandma Norma survived a rattlesnake bite and caught a stingray once with her father. She loved to read and play baseball in the streets with the boys. She delivered groceries on a bicycle. There was a real Mrs. Shaw at a real boarding house, and Grandma really did interrupt a phone call because of a fire on the stove. I heard the story of Alice the Ghost many times as a small child. I've even been to the house where Alice lived. It's called The Hermitage, and it has since

been moved and preserved in a beautiful way by distant
cousins. And just like Lily, Grandma did enter a summer
reading contest, although she came in second. In the real story,
the Beulah May Porter character won first place.

Hazel's character was entirely imagined. My grandmother
doesn't speak much about interracial interactions beyond
having Black housekeepers, fondly remembering one named
Martha who saved her life when she became ill. My motivation
in creating and telling Hazel's story was to show that courage
can be found anywhere you look, and that kindness and
empathy are, above all, the most important things we possess.
Hazel and Lily are different, not just in their skin color, but also
in their mannerisms and their personalities. But I believe, deep
in my soul, that two such different people can end up being the
best of friends and that fighting for friendship and justice is one
of the best ways we can show love for our fellow humans.

I hope I did Hazel's story justice. I know there's a lot of talk
out there about who has the right to tell what kind of stories,
and I do not pretend to understand the complete feelings or
thoughts of a young Black girl and her family living in the Jim
Crow South. I did a lot of reading during the writing and
rewriting of this book—history and memoir and fiction and
everything in between, and I hope that I have given Hazel an
authentic voice. I wanted to show the ways in which the girls
were similar, too; how humanity ties us together, how children
—despite their differences—have similar dreams, love to learn
and play, enjoy being left to just be a kid. And also, I wanted to
show how books can be such a point of connection, how they
can bring the unlikeliest of people together.

The prejudice portrayed throughout the story gives a small
picture of what life was like in the South during the 1940s.
Racism was rampant, Jim Crow laws were in full effect, and
hate crimes such as the fire at the boarding house were

committed by groups and individuals acting on their prejudices against Black people as well as Jewish people and other non-white people. Schools in South Carolina were not integrated until September of 1963, a full nine years after the historic Supreme Court case of *Brown vs. Board of Education*, which ruled school segregation to be unconstitutional. South Carolina, the first state to secede before the Civil War, was the last in the country to integrate public schools.

Due to rampant white supremacy and prejudice, job opportunities in the Jim Crow South were limited for Black people, mostly to service-related jobs. Many Black women like Hazel's Mama and Ma Maybelle worked in white homes or businesses cleaning, cooking, and minding children. My intention in having the Jackson women work these jobs in *Hand in Hand* was never to imply that service jobs were all that Black women were capable of, but to maintain a truth about history that career options were limited. There were, of course, Black teachers like Miss Grace and doctors like Doc Harding, but the majority of jobs available to Black people at the time were service jobs.

The books Lily and Hazel read together are some of my favorites, ones I read over and over as a child. The only exception is *The Hundred Dresses*, which I didn't find until I was teaching fourth grade. I read it aloud every single year to my classes. Also, *The Brownies' Book* in the story was a real publication, and full issues can be found online at http://childlit.unl.edu/topics/edi.brownies.html.

Throughout *Hand in Hand*, I used the words "Negro" and "colored" in order to stay true to the time. However, these words are not used today and are considered extremely offensive. The correct term, as of the writing of this book, is simply *Black* or *person of color*. And while we may have come a long way with our language, there is still a lot of racism and racial bias in America that we need to confront and fight against every day.

I'm grateful to come from a long line of writers. They may not have been traditionally published, but they were writers all the same. I have, in my possession, detailed memoirs from my grandmother and her father as well, which helped tremendously in the writing of this book. I'm so grateful they chose to write them down. The memories are precious to me, and I believe there is nothing more important that we can pass to our children than our stories.

FURTHER SUGGESTED READING

For middle graders

Clean Getaway by Nic Stone (2020)
Roll of Thunder, Hear My Cry by Mildred D. Taylor (1991)
The Watson's Go to Birmingham-1963 by Christopher Paul Curtis (2000)
Bud, Not Buddy by Christopher Paul Curtis (1999)
Stella by Starlight by Sharon M. Draper (2015)

For teens

Stamped: Racism, Antiracism, and You by Ibram X. Kendi and Jason Reynolds (2020)

For adults

Stamped from the Beginning: The Definitive History of Racist Ideas in America by Ibram X. Kendi (2016)
The Warmth of Other Suns: The Epic Story of America's Great Migration by Isabel Wilkerson (2010)
Caste: The Origins of Our Discontent by Isabel Wilkerson (2020)

ACKNOWLEDGMENTS

This book, like probably all books ever written, would not exist without a whole lot of people who cheered me on, read terrible draft after terrible draft, gave me excellent advice and reflection points, and challenged my thinking.

For Grandma Norma, for telling me your library contest story so many times it turned into an idea for an entire novel.

For my earliest readers: Aunt Heather and Aunt Lucy, your experience and knowledge about life and writing were invaluable to me and the writing of this book. Mom, Dad, Anna, Aunt Becky, and Kristin, thank you for taking time to go through this one and offer your thoughts. Heather, Megan, Jillian, Jessica, Gabi, Ashley, Mikaela, Kristy, Jillian, and Marie—your feedback was so important to me, so many things were revised because of you pushing me to make it better.

To my Uncle John and Aunt Amy, thank you for the publishing advice, for the checking in and enthusiasm through each step of the process.

To Rylee and Olivia—my very first middle grade readers,

your thoughts and questions were so important to me as I revised. I hope you love this final version.

To Kate, for braving a big, unknown writing conference with me and encouraging me to pitch my work. Thank you for saying yes to someone you barely knew.

To Amy—for not simply rejecting this messy manuscript but instead helping me improve it—and all the people at Metamorphosis, I'm so lucky to be part of a great literary agency. Your love for your authors is evident every day.

To my writing group: Jillian, Marie, and Dorothy—thank you for reading my words, thank you for trusting me with yours. And also—thank you for holding me accountable. I wouldn't be able to do this work without you.

To Erica, thank you for always believing that one day this would get published. It's finally here, and you never gave up hoping it would come.

To Alicia, my first editor, thank you for polishing this so that I could get it out to agents.

To Renee and Moninya, thank you for being amazing sensitivity readers, pointing out my blind spots and anywhere my writing was stereotypical or problematic. Your work is so important, and this novel would not be what it is without your valuable insight.

To Jodi and Twyla Beth, for believing in this one from the very beginning, for allowing me to grow and change as a person and also revise significant portions of this story to make sure I was honoring history and the people who lived it. I'm so grateful for your kindness and encouragement. I'm so lucky to be part of the Fawkes Press family.

To Ashley, for bringing Hazel and Lily to life so beautifully on the cover. Your work is stunning.

For the works of Ibram X. Kendi, Isabel Wilkerson, Jason Reynolds, and all others who are dedicating their life to educating us about the history of racism in this country and all the ways it has impacted us through the generations. I'm so grateful for your words; I pray every day that we are moving toward a more equitable society. And to Kaytee, for putting these books in my hands, reading them with me and learning alongside me, and for reading an early copy of *Hand in Hand*. I'm so grateful for your friendship.

Finally, for my husband and my babies. Hesston, McKinley, and Bradley, thank you for letting me dream, giving me the space and time to write, cheering for me, throwing quarantine book launch parties for me, all of it. I love you three to the moon.

ALSO BY KATIE PROCTOR

My Storied Year: a novel

Your Storied Year: a journal

Pen in Hand: a journal

If you enjoyed this book, please have an adult help you do one of the following:

- Leave a review on your favorite book review site
- Tell a friend about Hand in Hand and Katie Proctor
- Ask your local library to put Katie Proctor's work on the shelf
- Recommend Fawkes Press titles to your local bookstore

VISIT US ONLINE

WWW.KATIEPROCTORWRITES.COM

WWW.FAWKESPRESS.COM

FAWKES PRESS

ABOUT THE ARTIST

The beautiful cover art is by Ashley Aarons of AmaArt.
Ashley is originally from Kingston, Jamaica. The bulk of her creations are acrylic painting on canvas, but she is also a big fan of "the almighty undo" option allowed with digital art. BIPOC are her greatest inspiration, as she is intrigued by the similarities within the diversity. She intends for her art to show-case women of all races and shapes, and give them a platform to be seen and acknowledged. Through book illustrations she has helped bring to life characters who embody her inspiration, values, outlook, and hopes for a better future.

CPSIA information can be obtained
at www.ICGtesting.com
Printed in the USA
BVHW031007030621
608728BV00002B/114

9 781945 419546